MYSTERY EXPLOSION!

The Gun Lake Adventure Series

BOOK 2

by Johnnie Tuitel and Sharon Lamson

Cedar Tree
Publishing

MYSTERY EXPLOSION
Copyright 1998, 2000, 2005 by Johnnie Tuitel and Sharon E. Lamson

Published by Cedar Tree Publishing
1916 Breton Road, SE
Grand Rapids, MI 49506
1-888-302-7463 (toll free)
www.tapshoe.com

Third Printing

Cover and Illustration: Dan Sharp

Library of Congress Catalog-in-Publication Data
Lamson, Sharon E. 1948-
Tuitel, Johnnie, 1963-

cm.—(The Gun Lake Adventure Series)

Summary: First there is an explosion. Then an arrest is made that shocks the quiet town of Gun Lake. A stranger in town paves the way for another Gun Lake mystery and adventure. Friendship and loyalties are tested as Johnnie Jacobson and the Gun Lake kids try to find the answers to "Who did it?" and "Why?"

ISBN 0-9658075-1-7

[1. Adventure stories—Fiction 2. Mystery and detective stories—Fiction 3. Physically Handicapped—Children—Fiction 4. Michigan—Fiction]

I. Title   II. Series: Lamson Sharon E. 1948-, Tuitel, Johnnie, 1963

(The Gun Lake Adventure Series)

Dedication

To Korte St. John, a friend and colleague who has always gone above and beyond the call of duty. Without his tireless efforts, Alternatives In Motion would not be the organization it is today.

Also, to the silent one behind all that is done through Alternatives In Motion and Tap Shoe Productions. His creativity and guidance is priceless. I could not ask for a better business partner and friend. Thank you, George Ranville.

—JOHNNIE TUITEL

To my parents Frank and Eileen Eblen who have faithfully saved everything I ever wrote. Through good times and rough times, they have always been there for me, and their lives are a constant inspiration.

—SHARON E. LAMSON

Meet the Gun Lake Kids

Gun Lake, Michigan is where Johnnie and his friends live—a place where they have enjoyed many adventures.

Johnnie Jacobson

Eleven years old and full of adventure, Johnnie was born with cerebral palsy and uses a wheelchair to get around. He and his family moved to Gun Lake form California. The color of his dark-brown hair matches his eyes. He loves sports of all kinds—especially football.

Danny Randall

Blond, hazel eyes, and all-around sports buff, Danny loves being on the water. He is eleven years old and attends Gun Lake Middle School. With natural leadership skills and a "let's go get 'em" attitude, it's easy to see why he's Johnnies best friend.

Katy Randall

Like her older brother, blond-haired, green-eyed Katy enjoys being outdoors. She also loves reading and taking care of her cat. She's nine years old and attends Chief Noonday Elementary School.

Robyn Anderson

Robyn is spunky and very tall for her age—which is eleven. She likes her dark-brown hair to be kept short. She has brown eyes and tans easily in the Michigan sun. Competitive, smart and fun, Robyn enjoys being part of any adventure.

Nick Tysman

One phrase best describes ten-year-old Nick, and that is "easy going." He likes being outdoors, playing in sports and backpacking with his family out West. His brown hair and brown eyes make him look like he could almost be Johnnie's younger brother.

Joey Thomas

Joey's light brown hair and hazel green eyes, coupled wit his round face, make him look angelic. Openly curious about everything, Joey likes hangin gout with the other gun Lake kids. Like Katy, Joey is nine years old and attends Chief Noonday Elementary school.

Travis Hughes

Travis—the picture of the perfect athlete. His sandy-blond hair, blue eyes and tanned skin make him popular with the girls. When Johnnie came into town, Travis wasn't too sure he could "hang" with someone who used a wheelchair. He and Johnnie are friends—but not close.

Acknowledgment

We would like to acknowledge Heather True, a fifth-grade student at Excel Charter Academy in Grand Rapids, Michigan, who came up with the title of this book, Mystery Explosion.

TABLE OF CONTENTS

CHAPTER ONE

Tag! You're Out!

"I've been hit!" Johnnie yelled as he grabbed at his chest and toppled from his wheelchair to the ground. He looked up expecting someone to rush to his aid—but no one appeared. "I *always* get hit," he muttered, grabbing onto his wheelchair and hoisting himself into it again. He threw his SuperPower laser gun to the ground. "I give up on this game," he yelled. He gave the wheels on his wheelchair a hard push, rolled toward the sidewalk and headed for home.

"Don't you dare give up, Johnnie Jacobson!" eight-year-old Katy Randall yelled, as she stumbled out of the bushes. Her laser power pack was securely fastened to her chest and back. She tucked her blonde hair back under her baseball cap and stomped over to where Johnnie sat looking dejected. Green eyes flashing, she said, "Look, just because you have cerebral palsy and are in a wheelchair doesn't mean you can quit in the middle of a war."

"My disability has nothing to do with it," Johnnie

shouted. His dark brown eyes challenged Katy to say something else.

"Okay, lighten up, you guys," Katy's older brother Danny said as he ran toward them. He firmly gripped his own laser gun in his right hand. "This is just a game, remember?"

Danny, who was 11 years old—the same age as Johnnie—picked up his friend's plastic laser gun and handed it to him. Robyn Anderson emerged from behind one of the large oak trees that separated the Randalls' large backyard from the dense woods behind it. Dressed in her camouflage shorts, a tan T-shirt and a camouflage baseball-style cap, she blended in nicely with the trees and shrubs.

"What's going on?" Robyn asked, as she casually draped the strap of her laser gun over her shoulder.

"It's what's *not* going on," Katy said. "Johnnie wants to quit."

Just then 10-year-old Nick Tysman came running out from the woods. "Help!" he cried, waving his arms around wildly and moving his short legs as fast as he could. "Help!"

Everyone's attention turned toward Nick. He looked scared, and his face was red from running so hard. Danny ran out to meet him.

"What's wrong, Nick?" Danny asked as Nick nearly ran over him.

"It's—" Nick tried hard to talk between breaths."It's Joey!"

"What's wrong with Joey?" Robyn asked.

But Nick had doubled over trying to catch his breath.

Robyn's tall, lanky frame towered over Nick and she placed her hand firmly on his shoulder. "Nick," she said quietly but firmly, "tell us what's wrong with Joey."

Just then, a muffled voice called out from the woods. "Get me out of here!"

Nick straightened up and pointed toward the sound of the voice. "He's stuck!" he gasped.

Without waiting for further explanation, Katy, Danny and Robyn raced off toward the woods, leaving Johnnie to attend to Nick.

"Joey!" Danny yelled. "Where are you?"

"Over here!" His voice seemed to be coming from a deep hole.

"Keep talking," Robyn called out. "That way we can follow the sound of your voice."

Joey began counting as loudly as he could. "One...two...three..."

"I think he's over by the creek," Danny said as he whacked away at wild raspberry branches that had overgrown the path. "Watch out for the thorns," he warned Katy and Robyn, who were right behind him.

As the trio neared the creek, Robyn spotted Joey's leg protruding from a fallen hollow log. "He's over here!" she said.

Danny and Katy went to the front of the log and peered inside. There was Joey, still counting. "We're here, Joey," Danny announced.

Joey lifted his head and saw his two friends looking in at him. "I'm stuck!" he said.

"Well, that's obvious," Katy said. Then she looked at Robyn who was at the other end of the log. "Can you pull him out?"

Robyn grabbed Joey's legs and pulled but Joey was wedged in so tightly, the log moved with him.

I've got an idea," said Danny. "Katy, you and I will hold the front of the log and pull one way while Robyn pulls Joey's legs the other way."

"Sounds like a plan to me," Robyn said. Then to Joey she said, "Don't worry, we'll get you out of there."

"On the count of three," Danny said, "We'll all pull. One...two...three!"

Robyn dug her heels into the dirt and pulled with all her might. Katy and Danny each grabbed a side of the log and pulled in the opposite direction. With a loud "oof," Robyn tumbled backward and landed in a pile of dead leaves—with Joey landing beside her.

"Wow!" Joey exclaimed. "I thought I was going to be stuck in there forever." His normally rosy cheeks were bright red and perspiration ran down his face. "Thanks," he added, as Robyn helped him to his feet.

Just then the kids heard a familiar voice calling, "Danny, Katy, Robyn, Joey! Where are you?"

"That sounds like Kort!" Danny said.

Kort Sinclair was the chief mechanic for Chester Faraday who owned a special race car called a dragster. Chester's son Scott raced it. Only a few years ago, Chester sat in the driver's seat, but a crash into a wall injured his spinal cord high up on his back. His injury caused him to become a *quadriplegic*—someone whose legs are paralyzed and whose arms are either completely or partially paralyzed.

The kids enjoyed watching the races at the Gun Lake race track. Johnnie especially enjoyed having wheelchair races with Chester, though Chester always won because he used a electric-powered chair while Johnnie had to use his hands to move his chair.

When Johnnie showed particular interest in dragsters, Kort was more than willing to share his knowledge with him. Johnnie learned that dragsters use nitromethane for fuel because it is highly explosive. "The more combustible or explosive a fuel is, the more power is released," Kort had said.

These sleek-looking cars are raced on straight asphalt that is 1320 feet long (commonly called a quarter-mile track) at speeds of up to 300 mph. Much to Johnnie's delight, he learned that there are junior dragsters that race on eighth-mile tracks.

Because the cars achieve such high speeds in a relatively short period of time, huge parachutes are ejected from the back to slow them down after they reach the finish line.

Right now, Danny was wondering what Kort was doing in the woods calling out his name. "We're over here," Danny yelled. Kort's reddish-blond hair glistened in the patchy sunlight, making it easy to spot him.

Kort trampled over the path, quickly making his way to them. "Johnnie told me Joey was in trouble," he said, worry reflecting in his green eyes.

"Well, he *was* in trouble," Katy said. "But we managed to pull him out of it."

Kort knelt on one knee and eyed Joey from head to toe. "Hmmm," he said. "You *look* okay. What happened?"

Joey began moving the dirt around in front of him with the toe of his shoe. He watched as the sandy soil gave way to the pressure of his shoe. Then slowly, he raised his eyes to look at Kort.

"Um," he began. "I was looking for a really cool spot where I could ambush everybody as they ran past me. Well, I guess I was the one who got ambushed."

The corners of his mouth curled upward slightly. He had to bite his lower lip to keep from laughing out loud. "I'm sorry," he said. "I didn't mean to get everyone so upset."

Kort hugged Joey as he gave way to a big belly laugh. "We're just glad you're not hurt. I'll have to work with you on finding 'cool' but safe places to hide in ambush!"

As everyone prepared to leave, Johnnie came wheeling down the path with Nick walking behind him. Johnnie was breathing hard from pushing his chair down an uneven, dirt path. "Hey!" he shouted, "What's going on?"

"Joey was stuck in a log but we got him out," Robyn answered. "He wanted to ambush us with his laser gun."

"Like I'd really push myself in here to play laser tag," Johnnie said. He slapped the laser gun that was resting in his lap.

The other kids walked on ahead as Kort pushed

Johnnie back up the path toward the Randalls' backyard.

"What was that all about?" Kort asked.

Johnnie was going to pretend he didn't know what Kort was talking about, but he was feeling too disgusted with himself to play games with his friend. Johnnie hung his head. He felt like he was going to cry.

"Kort," Johnnie said softly, "I don't want to end up feeling sorry for myself just because I'm in a wheelchair. Most of the time, it really doesn't matter. But at times like this—you know—when you have to be quick and able to hide—well let's just say I may as well put a target on my back that says 'Shoot Me.'"

"Oh," Kort answered, smiling to himself, "so *that's* it. You just need to learn some strategy."

"What do you mean?" Johnnie asked.

"When I was in the Vietnam War, we American soldiers had to learn how to adapt to our surroundings. Our enemy already knew the jungles. They had lived in the tropical conditions and were used to the insects, animal life and plants. We had to figure out ways to protect ourselves—we had to learn strategy."

"And so you're saying I have to learn ways to protect myself?" Johnnie said.

"Exactly! Protect yourself and at the same time, be able to put your enemy at a disadvantage."

"Well, the Gun Lake kids aren't really my enemies," Johnnie said. "I mean, we're friends—in a club together."

"Okay," said Kort, "Let's call them *opponents* then. The name of this game is to tag as many of your opponents as you can without getting tagged yourself, right?"

"Right," Johnnie said. "When someone tags us, we're supposed to yell out, 'I've been hit.' We each keep track of how many times we've been tagged. So far, I've been tagged about a zillion times."

Kort stopped pushing Johnnie and walked around to the front of his wheelchair. Kneeling down, Kort looked Johnnie in the eyes knowingly. "You'll just have to hide in Danny's garage," he said.

"What? Hide in the garage. No way! I'd rather not play than just hide," Johnnie said.

"Oh, you'll be playing," Kort said, a mischievous smile inching across his face. "You'll be watching for the enemy—er, I mean, your opponents in the side mirror of the Randalls' van parked in the garage."

"What then?" Johnnie almost whispered. He leaned forward in his wheelchair and looked around to see if anyone was within earshot.

"Then you aim at the reflection of their laser pack in the mirror and fire!"

Johnnie looked confused so Kort continued, "With a laser gun, you can shoot at your target using a mirror. The laser beam ricochets off the mirror and hits the target."

"Wow!" Johnnie said. "How'd you learn all that stuff?"

"I worked with experimental lasers while in the military," Kort said.

"I didn't know that," Johnnie said.

"There's a lot about me you don't know," Kort replied. "But for now, I think we'd better get you back in the game over at the Randalls' house."

When Kort and Johnnie showed up in Danny and Katy's backyard, the other kids were just beginning to unhook their laser packs.

"Hey!" Johnnie shouted. "What are you guys doing? Aren't we going to play laser tag?"

"I thought you didn't want to play anymore," Katy said, her hands on her hips.

"Oh, I was just feeling sorry for myself," Johnnie said. "I just needed time to think of a little strategy."

Katy sighed then began fastening her laser pack back on again. Danny just smiled then said, "Okay everyone—take your places!"

Johnnie waited until everyone had scrambled away before he quickly headed for the Randalls' garage. He chose a spot a few feet behind the van's left side mirror. He stayed as close to the garage wall as possible so no one would see him. Then he picked up his laser gun and waited.

Before long, Nick came into view. Johnnie carefully aimed at Nick's laser pack. "I sure hope this works," Johnnie muttered to himself. Slowly, Johnnie squeezed the trigger and the next thing he knew, Nick was yelling, "Hey! I've been hit!"

Johnnie chuckled to himself. Soon Danny came into view—and he too was zapped by Johnnie's laser. "Who did that?" Danny cried. By the end of the afternoon, Johnnie had chalked up 16 tags using his mirror strategy.

It was almost time for dinner so the kids decided to end the game. Everyone headed toward the front yard. "Where's Johnnie?" Joey asked. No one seemed to know, so they all went around front to wait.

Johnnie waited until everyone had left before he abandoned his hiding place. When he joined the others, they were amazed that he hadn't been tagged even once. They were even more surprised to learn that he had tagged them 16 times!

"Where were you hiding?" Robyn asked.

"That's a military secret," Johnnie answered.

CHAPTER TWO

Getting Ready for the Big Race

When Johnnie awoke on Sunday morning, all he could think about was how well the strategy worked that he and Kort had talked about on Saturday.

As he lay in bed, a warm morning breeze wandered in from off the lake. It was going to be another hot, humid summer day in West Michigan.

Then, just as if someone had poured cold water on him, Johnnie sat up in bed. "The qualifications! We're going to the Faradays' private race track after church!" Johnnie exclaimed.

Sunday afternoons usually found Johnnie and his family eating a picnic lunch on the shores of Gun Lake. But not *this* Sunday.

Scott Faraday was going to test run his dragster. Kort had invited the Jacobsons to watch. Johnnie loved every part of racing. He loved the smells of fuel, oil and the rubber from the tires. He loved the deep rumble of the engines. He could even feel the vibrations through his wheelchair. And he loved to watch the dragsters blast their way down the track.

The crowd's wild cheering and obvious love of the sport was contagious. Johnnie found himself fascinated with how fast the pit crew worked, with the bright colors of the dragsters and the sponsors' names and logos that decorated each car. He also loved to see the racers in their racing suits and helmets.

Like many race car owners and drivers, the Faradays owned a private track and garage. It was at this garage that Kort spent most of his time tuning and fine-tuning the many parts of the dragster's engine, clutch and fuel system. Everything had to be in perfect running order before it could be entered into a race.

On this particular day, Kort and his crew were working hard to get the Faraday dragster ready for next Saturday's big race. Scott Faraday had yet to win a race. His father had won many in years past. It wasn't that Scott didn't like racing. He did—but as a spectator, not a driver.

When Johnnie and his family arrived at the race track, Johnnie was surprised to see Travis Hughes there. Travis was one of the Gun Lake kids Johnnie played with—though the two of them weren't exactly "best friends."

When Johnnie and his family had first moved from California to Michigan, all of the neighborhood kids—Robyn, Danny, Katy, Nick and Joey—had been very eager to meet him and welcome him into the club—all except Travis, that is.

Travis was a natural athlete and was used to being in charge of things. Seeing Johnnie in a wheelchair and learning that he had cerebral palsy made Travis feel uncomfortable. He avoided Johnnie and made rude remarks under his breath.

When the other kids encouraged Johnnie to go through a club initiation, Travis didn't believe Johnnie would make it. The initiation turned into a real life-and-death adventure, however, and Travis was impressed by Johnnie's ability to handle a very danger-ous situation at the old McGruther barn at Gun Lake.

Since that time, Johnnie and Travis' friendship had begun to grow. Though still a little uncomfortable around each other, they each respected the other and were friendly.

Johnnie watched as Travis and Kort walked toward him. "Hi, Johnnie," Kort said. "Travis and I were just going over to the garage to make some final adjustments on the dragster before we tow it out to the track. Want to come along?"

Johnnie glanced at Travis to see what his reaction would be to Kort's invitation. Travis cocked his head to one side, shrugged and said, "Sure, why not come along?"

Kort and Travis strolled alongside Johnnie's chair as Johnnie pushed toward the garage. "By the way," Johnnie said to Kort, "what kind of experimental lasers did you work on when you were in the army? I didn't even know they had lasers back then."

Kort laughed. "Most people think lasers are something new. Actually, Gordon Gould, an American scientist invented the laser in 1958. Two years later another scientist, T. H. Maiman built the first working model. By the way, did you know that the word *laser* is actually an acronym?"

"A what?" Travis asked. He didn't know why Johnnie and Kort were talking about lasers at a race track but it was beginning to sound interesting.

"An acronym is a name made up of the first letters of words used in an official title—like NASA, which stands for National Aeronautics and Space Administration, or a product, like *laser*," Kort answered.

"Well, then, what do the letters L-A-S-E-R stand for?" Johnnie asked.

"Light Amplification by Stimulated Emission of Radiation. Light can come out of a laser in a narrow beam that can be focused down to less than a one-thousandth of an inch in diameter. These beams are so powerful that they can be used to drill tiny holes in diamonds in just minutes, where the old methods took days."

"What makes them so powerful?" Travis asked.

"Well, for one thing," Kort said, "they travel in a straight line and are very accurate. When you use a flashlight, does the beam stay in a straight, narrow line or does it spread out?"

"It spreads out," Travis said.

"Exactly! Light from a flashlight gets wider as it travels. Therefore, there is less light at the end of the beam than there is at the source," Kort said. "Laser light is different. It follows a parallel beam and stays narrow. The amount of light stays pretty much the same from the beginning of the beam to its end. A laser beam is sharper and purer than regular light and can travel great distances without losing its power."

"Wow!" said Johnnie. "Did you ever use any real laser guns?"

Kort looked at Johnnie and smiled. "Let's just say I've had a lot of experience with them."

"What's all this talk about lasers anyway?" Travis wanted to know.

"We were playing laser tag yesterday at Danny and Katy's. Kort showed up and taught me some strategy so I wouldn't be a sitting duck all the time," Johnnie said.

By this time they had reached the garage and all discussion switched to race cars. From the moment Johnnie wheeled inside the massive garage, he couldn't stop looking at the Faradays' dragster.

It was approximately 300 inches long. The engine was mounted in the back and was out in the open. The rear tires were large and wide. Just in front of the engine was the semi-enclosed cockpit where the driver sat. The body was tapered like a long arrow—starting out wider in the back and then stretching to almost a point in the front. The front wheels were smaller and thinner.

Because race cars were so expensive to make and keep running, race car owners asked corporations like Pennzoil, Mopar, McDonalds or even Victoria Salsa to sponsor them. In return for the money they donated, the car would be painted with the sponsor's logo and name. The Faraday car was sponsored by Hollingsworth Oil, and displayed the colorful red and yellow Hollingsworth logo on a white background.

Johnnie thought about Scott's fiery red hair. To him,

it was a perfect match for his red and yellow helmet and racing suit. Once, after Johnnie had witnessed his first drag race, he had asked Scott why the cars didn't race around an oval track, like they do in stock car racing.

Scott's answer was, "These cars are built to go in a straight line, not to go around curves. The whole point in drag racing is to see who can accelerate the fastest from a standing start. We try to cover the distance of the track in the shortest time possible."

Johnnie and Travis watched as the pit crew checked the tires and every centimeter of the dragster. Kort had a checklist and, as things were tightened, tweaked or examined, he made notes.

"Is she ready to roll, Kort?" Chester Faraday's loud, booming voice echoed off the garage walls as he maneuvered his power wheelchair over to where his chief mechanic stood.

"She's as ready as she'll ever be, Chester," Kort said.

"I hope so, Kort. Mr. Hollingsworth has made it very clear that he's considering pulling his money away from us and sponsoring someone else. We've got to start winning races."

Kort swallowed hard, then took a deep breath. "It's not the car," he said evenly. "We've never had a mechanical failure that cost us a race."

Chester's face reddened. He looked as if he were going to yell at Kort, but then he suddenly drew in a deep breath and let out a long sigh.

"You're saying that we need a new driver?" Chester asked. "You think I don't know that Scott doesn't like to race—that he's doing it just to please me because he feels sorry for me. Sometimes, Kort, I think it would be better if the car would get totaled, and that would be the end of it. I could collect the insurance and open up a spare parts store some-where. And Scott—" Mr. Faraday didn't continue.

"Surely, you don't want Scott to crash the car?" Kort asked, alarmed.

Chester looked up at his long-time friend. "Of course not, Kort. You know me better than that. One 'crash dummy' in the family is enough. Maybe I ought to just take a stick of dynamite to her."

Kort frowned. Chester saw the look of concern on his face and then laughed. "Oh, come on, Kort. Where's your sense of humor. I'd never do anything like that and you know it. Though if we lose Hollingsworth Oil, I don't know who else will back us up."

Johnnie and Travis tried to shrink into the back-ground while Kort and Mr. Faraday were having this discussion. They felt guilty at having overheard as much as they did.

Out of the corner of his eye, Johnnie saw something move in the doorway. He turned his head quickly just in time to see Scott Faraday turn and walk away.

"Oh, no!" Johnnie whispered to Travis and pointed toward the door. "I think Scott heard what his father said."

"He must feel awful," Travis said.

"Do you think we should try to catch up with Scott and talk to him?" Johnnie asked.

"He knows you better than he does me," Travis said. "Why don't you go after him. I'll stay here until they tow the car out to the track."

Johnnie didn't know if he could catch up with Scott or not but he decided to give it a try. He pushed the wheel-rims of his chair hard. Once he cleared the doorway, Johnnie sped out onto the wide asphalt driveway. He squinted in the bright sunlight as he quickly scanned the area hoping he could spot Scott. But he needn't have rushed. Scott was sitting on a bench just outside the garage.

"Whoa, there!" Scott said, as Johnnie nearly whizzed by him. "Where are you going so fast?"

"Oh, hi Scott," Johnnie said, trying to act as if nothing important was happening. "Actually, I was looking for you."

"Well, you found me. What's up?"

Johnnie didn't know where to begin. If he asked him point blank if he had heard what his father had said, and if Scott hadn't heard anything, then he would want to know what was going on. *Strategy*, Johnnie thought to himself. *Kort says you gotta have strategy.*

"So, I was just wondering if you were ready for today's qualification runs," Johnnie said. He smiled weakly at Scott.

"I'm as ready as I'll ever be," Scott said.

"Well, I was just wondering if you thought the *dragster* was ready," Johnnie said. He knew he was trying to buy time so he could think of a better way to find out if Scott had overheard his dad's comments.

Scott smiled at Johnnie. "Well, according to my father, your *first* question is probably more important than the second—am *I* ready."

So he *had* heard. Johnnie looked down at the pavement. He suddenly felt embarrassed. "I'm sorry, Scott," he finally blurted out. "I wasn't sure if you had heard—you know—what your father said."

"Don't feel bad, Johnnie," Scott said. "He's right. I hate racing. I don't do it because I feel sorry for him, I do it because I want him to be proud of me. I'm just lousy at it, that's all. I know Mr. Hollingsworth is putting pressure on us to come through with a couple of wins. Believe me, Johnnie, I don't try to lose. I guess that fire that is supposed to burn in every race driver's heart, doesn't even flicker for me."

"What would you rather do?" Johnnie asked.

"I like my guitar and I like backpacking in Colorado. I've even written a couple songs about the mountains and streams—sort of a songwriter wannabe," he said, and then he laughed.

"Wow! You've actually written some songs? Have you tried to publish any of them?" Johnnie asked.

Scott shook his head no. "Not enough time to do that," he said. "Too many races to drive." As he got up to head for the track, he muttered, "If I had a stick of dynamite, I sure know what I'd blow up with it."

Johnnie was sure Scott didn't mean for him to hear that last remark. With mixed feelings, Johnnie headed back into the garage, and was just in time to see the tow truck being hooked up to the tail end of the dragster.

"So there you are," Kort said as he saw Johnnie wheel back into the garage. "You're just in time. Travis, you can ride with Jake in the tow truck, and Johnnie, you're with me in the pickup truck. I'll just fold your chair and secure it in the flatbed. Then it's off to the races—well, at least to the test run!" He laughed at his own joke.

As he and Kort followed after the tow truck, Johnnie wondered about what Chester and Scott had said. *Maybe it* would *be better if the dragster blew up*, Johnnie thought. He shook his head slightly as if to clear his thoughts. *No*, he argued with himself, *that would not be better. It would be better if Scott could be honest with his dad and if Chester could simply find another racer before it's too late.*

CHAPTER THREE

Meltdown!

For the next week, Johnnie and the Gun Lake kids entertained themselves playing laser tag. No one discovered Johnnie's hiding place, even though Travis had come close a couple of times.

Meanwhile, Gun Lake was gearing up for the big race. Banners were being hung across the main streets. The newspapers all over West Michigan displayed advertisements. The local radio station was set up at the race track, ready to cover the day's events.

Once in awhile, Johnnie's thoughts wandered back to the conversation he had overheard between Kort and Mr. Faraday. He also pondered what Scott had said. All this talk about blowing up the racer gave Johnnie an eerie feeling.

He told Travis about his conversation with Scott, and Travis shrugged his shoulders and sighed. "Stay out of it," he warned. "It's none of your business."

Reluctantly, Johnnie had to agree. After all, what could

he do? It really was between Mr. Faraday and his son.

On Thursday evening, Kort called Johnnie and asked if he would like to go to the track with him Friday morning. "You can watch me do a final test run before the big race on Saturday," he said.

"You're going to do the test run and not Scott?" Johnnie asked, surprised.

"Sure! I know how to drive one of these babies," Kort said. "What do you say?"

"Cool!" Johnnie said.

Friday's sunrise looked like a faint gray glow as moisture from Lake Michigan filtered in. By the time it was 8 o'clock, however, the sun had burned off the mist and the blue sky rolled out its welcome mat. Another sunny day! The lake breeze felt cool against Johnnie's face. He peeked out the window and saw his mother weeding her herb garden. Johnnie didn't especially like gardening. But he did enjoy rubbing the leaves of the herbs between his fingers and then smelling his fingers. Herbs like lemon balm and lemon verbena smelled just like the fruit after which they were named.

Mrs. Jacobson's garden also included oregano, basil, thyme, rosemary and other herbs she used in her kitchen. "I just love the way things grow in this sandy soil," she would often say.

Of course "things" included weeds, which fortunately pulled out of the ground easily because the soil was so sandy. As Johnnie watched his mother work, he thought she looked happy—in her own little herbal world.

He laughed lightly as he got out of bed. Today *he* would be in his own little racing world with Kort.

Shortly after breakfast, Kort's truck pulled up in Johnnie's driveway. Johnnie wheeled himself out the door and down the ramp that led to the driveway. Mrs. Jacobson came around the side of the house, her bushel basket full of weeds. "Hi, Kort," she said. "Is it going to be just you and Johnnie down at the Faradays' track today?"

"Yes," Kort said. "I'm going to make a few minor adjustments on the car and then make a couple test runs. We should be home shortly after lunch."

"Isn't that a little dangerous?" she asked. "If something should happen—like you crashed or something—who would be there to help you?"

"Aw, Mom," Johnnie whined.

Kort interrupted. "That's a good point, Mrs. Jacobson. I'll give Johnnie my cellular phone. If something happens, all he has to do is dial 9-1-1 and help will be on the way. Will that put your mind at ease?"

Mrs. Jacobson looked at her son's pleading eyes. For one very long moment, Johnnie was afraid she was going to say no. But then she chuckled and said, "Well, okay."

Johnnie let out a huge sigh of relief and then said, "Well, Kort, we'd better get going." *Before she thinks of something else,* he thought to himself.

Kort helped Johnnie transfer from his wheelchair into the pickup truck's cab and then loaded the wheelchair into the back. Waving goodbye to Mrs. Jacobson, Johnnie and Kort headed for the test track.

"Well, Johnnie, the big race is tomorrow. I sure hope Scott at least places this time."

Johnnie glanced at Kort. His face looked grim.

"If Scott doesn't win," Johnnie began, "will that Hollingsworth guy take his money away from Mr. Faraday and give it to someone else?"

Surprised by Johnnie's comment, Kort asked, "What made you ask that question?"

Johnnie shifted his glance away from Kort's face and looked out the window. Finally, he blurted, "I'm sorry, Kort. I didn't *mean* to hear what you and Mr. Faraday were talking about. I mean, he just came in and started talking, and Travis and I didn't know what to do."

Kort sighed and wiped his forehead with the back of his hand. "I'm sorry you had to hear all that," Kort said. "Racing is a lot of fun. The crowds, the beautiful cars, the pit crews hustling about—all lots of fun. But there's also the reality of racing—you have to win to stay in the game. If a car doesn't have a sponsor, it gets very expensive for the owner."

"I thought all the money from the ticket sales would be enough," Johnnie said.

"The money from the tickets goes toward keeping the racetrack in good shape and paying the prize money," Kort said. "Money to buy new tires and car parts, pay the pit crew and put fuel and oil into the car comes from sponsors. Mr. Faraday helps out with some of those costs, but it's much too expensive for him to do it all alone."

"Well, then, what does the sponsor get out of it?" Johnnie asked.

"Advertising! People see the sponsor's name and logo painted all over the car. Cars are known by their sponsors. The Faraday car is called what?"

"I guess I've always heard it called the 'Hollingsworth Oil' car," Johnnie replied.

"Exactly! And when you're at a gas station and see a can of Hollingsworth Oil sitting on a shelf, you think of the Hollingsworth Oil car, right?"

"Right!" Johnnie said.

"But if the Hollingsworth Oil car keeps losing, do you think you're going to want to put Hollingsworth Oil in your car?" Kort asked.

Johnnie thought for a moment. "Oh, I get it," he said. "People associate the car with the product."

"Yes—especially if the product has something to do with cars."

"But Kort," Johnnie continued, "you said the fact that the car was losing races didn't have anything to do with mechanical problems."

"Sponsors don't care what the problem is. To a sponsor—just like to the spectators—it's all about winning and losing."

"Do you think Scott loses on purpose?" Johnnie asked.

"I don't know," Kort said. "I know Scott isn't happy being a race driver. His heart isn't in it. Maybe he isn't losing on purpose—just subconsciously."

"Subcon—? What does *that* mean?" Johnnie asked.

"Subconsciously," Kort said. "It means doing or saying something and not being really aware of why you're doing it. For example, Scott hates racing. So maybe he *wants* to lose, only he really doesn't know it on a conscious level. He isn't thinking, 'I want to lose this race.' But his subconscious is thinking it."

"And so his subconscious takes over his actions?" Johnnie asked.

"I'm no psychologist," Kort answered, "but I think that's how it works sometimes."

"Wow! Cool!" Johnnie said.

Johnnie fixed his gaze on the lush green hills as he and Kort drove south on Marsh Road toward the test track. The road took them past West Gun Lake. Johnnie was fascinated with the names of the various islands and coves associated with the lake. Names like "Goat Island," "Gun Colony" and "England's Point" stirred Johnnie's adventuresome spirit. He wished Kort would turn on Wildwood Road and then north on Yankee Springs Road so they could drive through a place called "Devil's Soupbowl." Huge holes dotted the landscape there. People believed the holes were caused by either the glaciers or by meteorites, but no one knew for sure.

As the scenery sped by, Johnnie thought about Kort's words—that maybe Scott wanted to lose, subconsciously. He wondered if he ever did things subconsciously. Thoughts of everything he heard at the Faraday track plus what he and Kort had just discussed filled his mind. Before he knew it, Kort had pulled up to the gate that led to the Faradays' garage.

The entire property was enclosed with an electric fence. To get through the gate, Kort had to enter a code onto a small number pad. Once the correct seven digits were entered, the gate automatically opened. A motion detector monitored the truck passing through the gate. Once the gate was cleared, the heavy metal doors closed quickly.

Besides the electric fence and security code, video cameras with powerful lenses were mounted on top of the garage. These cameras constantly scanned the gate and the surrounding area, feeding pictures into a computer. A special security unit monitored the pictures at an outside location. If trouble was spotted, they activated a security alert that was directly connected to the local dispatch unit. Police were notified immediately.

After Johnnie and Kort had cleared the entrance, they made their way to the garage. It had to be opened by a special remote—similar to a garage door opener. The huge doors opened to reveal the highly polished Hollingsworth Oil dragster.

Kort unloaded Johnnie's wheelchair then transferred Johnnie out of the truck. "I'm just going to make a slight adjustment to the fuel system," Kort said. "Then

I want to check over a few other minor details. We should be able to tow the car out to the track within 15 minutes. Do you want something cold to drink?"

"Got any cola?" Johnnie asked.

"Here," Kort said, handing Johnnie some change. "Go over to the vending machine just outside the garage and get us both something."

When Johnnie returned a few minutes later, Kort was just finishing up his fuel-system adjustment. "Just a couple more quick checks, and I think we'll be ready," Kort said as Johnnie handed him his drink.

Johnnie watched Kort tighten bolts, check the pressure in the tires and give it a professional but quick "once-over."

"I think we're ready to hook it up to the tow truck," Kort said at last. "I'll haul us and the car out to the track. Then I'll help you get situated in the stands where you'll be able to see everything."

Johnnie watched Kort put on his racing suit. It wasn't as colorful as Scott's but it did have the Hollingsworth Oil logo stamped on the back. Kort's name was neatly embroidered on the right, front pocket.

"Why can't you do the test run in your regular clothes?" Johnnie asked.

"The driver needs to be as protected as possible,"

Kort answered. "The suit is made of flame retardant material that won't burn as quickly, in case of an accident. Plus I'll be wearing special shoes and gloves, as well as a helmet—all designed to protect me, just in case. Even in test runs, things can happen. I'm sure you've heard the phrase, 'safety first'."

Noticing the worried look on Johnnie's face, Kort added, "Rarely does anything bad happen. But the rules say I have to wear this special protective gear."

Johnnie felt somewhat relieved. "Just like I'm supposed to wear my seat belt when I'm in my wheelchair," Johnnie said. "Only sometimes I don't. And once my chair tipped over and I rolled out of it!"

"You got it, Johnnie. Even in wheelchairs you have to remember that phrase—"

"Safety first!" Johnnie said, smiling.

Kort finished hooking up the dragster and then he and Johnnie drove to the track. He first made sure Johnnie was comfortable in the spectator stands. Then Kort hauled the car over to the track, positioned it on the track and unhooked the tow truck. A fuel container was located at the pit area. Kort used it to fuel the car.

Next, Johnnie watched Kort put on his gloves and helmet. He then climbed into the cockpit. In a few seconds, the dragster's powerful engine roared to life.

Kort hadn't bothered to activate the lights on the track called the "Christmas tree." The Christmas tree was a tall pole, on which sets of red, yellow and green lights were attached. The lights stuck out from each side of the pole, making it looks similar to a tree. When the lights flashed green, it meant *go*.

Kort revved the engine a few times. In a few seconds, the dragster's rear tires spun, burning the rubber. Kort had told Johnnie that this was called a "burnout." This heated the tires so they could grip the track better. Johnnie watched as the tires spun against the asphalt and suddenly propelled the dragster down the quarter-mile track. Johnnie leaned forward against the guard rail so he could see the parachute eject from the back of the car.

"Awesome!" Johnnie said. He clapped and cheered. Kort shut off the engine, climbed out of the cockpit and began walking back along the track.

Johnnie yelled as loudly as he could, "You won! You won!"

As Kort approached the stands, he smiled at Johnnie. "I'm not sure I *would* have won. It just didn't feel right. I'm going to check that fuel system again.

You wait here while I go back to the garage to get my checklist and toolbox. I'll only be a minute."

"Sure," Johnnie said. "I'll be fine."

Johnnie watched as Kort climbed into the tow truck and sped off to the garage. "I bet I could race a car," he said. "I know regular cars have hand controls for people with disabilities who can't use their legs and feet. I wonder if race cars could have hand controls." Johnnie sat back in his seat and stared at the race track. He was in the middle of an action-packed, racing daydream, when he was jarred to reality by a thunderous BOOM!

The sound shook the stands and Johnnie fell out of his seat. He scrambled to the guard rail and pulled himself up. As he looked down the track, all he could see was massive billows of flames and black smoke. Johnnie could feel the heat from the flames.

He stared at the fire, unable to move. With much effort, he forced himself to look away. "Where's Kort's phone?" he cried, frantically.

Johnnie pulled himself back into his seat. With trembling fingers, he dialed 9-1-1. When the dispatch operator answered, all Johnnie could say was, "It just blew up."

"What blew up?" the operator asked calmly.

"The Hollingsworth Oil dragster," Johnnie muttered. Without thinking, he let the phone drop to the ground as he watched the dragster burn.

And then his mind went to Kort. Where was he?

CHAPTER FOUR

A Mystery to Solve

"Kort! Kort!" Johnnie yelled. He looked around frantically for his friend. Then he spotted him speeding toward the dragster in his own pickup truck. Johnnie watched him jump out of the truck with a huge fire extinguisher in his hand. He wasn't wearing the racing suit anymore.

"No! Don't!" Johnnie yelled, though he knew Kort couldn't hear him. He was sure the flames would somehow leap out and catch Kort's clothes on fire. Johnnie began screaming. He yelled so loudly that he didn't hear the sirens of the police cars and fire engines as they sped down the road toward the gate.

The security unit activated the gate by remote control and the gates swung open to let the emergency vehicles in. Johnnie watched the firemen use canisters of CO_2 to smother the flames. One fireman rushed over to Kort and led him away from the track.

Then he saw Kort point toward the stands. Several police officers got into a cruiser and quickly drove toward the area where Johnnie was sitting.

"Are you all right, Johnnie?" one of the officers called out. The officers ran toward him.

Johnnie merely nodded his head. He tried to speak but the words would not come out. He began to cry.

"It's going to be okay," one officer said. "Your friend is fine. Apparently, he wasn't in the car when it blew."

Johnnie tore his gaze from the scene of the explosion and focused his attention on the officers. "No he wasn't," Johnnie said softly. "Kort was in the garage. Said he had to go get some special tools to fix something in the fuel system. I was just sitting here—thinking about being a race car driver someday—when I heard the explosion."

"Are you hurt in any way?" the officer asked.

"No, I'm fine. I just want to go home." Johnnie wiped at his eyes.

"Johnnie!" Kort's voice sounded frantic. "Johnnie! Are you okay?"

Johnnie looked up to see Kort running on the track toward him. His face was smudged with soot and sweat. He was at Johnnie's side in a minute—hugging him. Johnnie could hear Kort's heart pounding through his shirt.

"Oh, Kort! What happened?" Johnnie cried.

"I don't know, Johnnie. I just don't know!" Kort's voice trailed off.

By now the flames were extinguished and the firemen were examining the wreckage. The once brightly painted dragster was charred. The smell of oil and rubber filled the air.

"Johnnie, where's the cellular phone I gave you?" Kort asked.

"It should be around here somewhere," Johnnie said as he looked around. "I used it to call 9-1-1, and then I think I dropped it."

Here it is," one of the officers said, handing Kort the phone. "It was on the ground below the stand."

Kort looked at Johnnie and smiled. "Good thinking," he said. "In spite of everything that was going on, you thought to call for help. I'm proud of you."

Johnnie managed a smile. "When can I go home?" he asked.

"I have to stay here and call Mr. Faraday. I'll probably have to talk to the fire chief. He's got his crew investigating what's left of that car now—to see if they can figure out what caused the explosion. But I'll call your mother and see if she can come pick you up."

"No need for that," said the officer. "My partner and

I can take him home. It doesn't look like there's any criminal activity here, and no one's hurt—so we're going to head back to town."

"You'll have to get his wheelchair out of the back of the tow truck," said Kort. "It folds up and should fit easily in your trunk."

By the time Johnnie got home, he was exhausted. His mother thanked the officers and helped Johnnie into the house. "What on earth happened?" his mother asked. "Are you sure Kort is all right?"

"Kort's fine, Mom," Johnnie answered. He transferred out of his wheelchair and flopped onto the living room sofa. "Can you just turn on a video or something? I just want to hang out awhile."

"I'll bring you something cold to drink," Mrs. Jacobson said. But by the time she had returned from the kitchen, Johnnie was asleep.

When Johnnie awoke, it was almost dinnertime. He sat up, found the remote control to the television, and pressed the button to turn it on. He was about to do some channel surfing when he saw Kort's face on the screen.

"Hey, Mom!" Johnnie yelled. "Kort's on TV!"

Mrs. Jacobson hurried from the kitchen and sat beside her son on the sofa. One of the local newsmen was interviewing Kort at the track. The blackened remains of the dragster were clearly visible behind them.

"This is Warren Reynolds, from TV 8 News, reporting live from the Faraday test track. Earlier this afternoon the Hollingsworth Oil dragster, owned by Chester Faraday, was destroyed in an explosion. Here with me is Kort Sinclair, the chief mechanic who was testing the car shortly before the incident." He then turned toward Kort and asked, "Where exactly were you when the car blew up?"

"I was back at the garage," he said. "I had just finished doing my test run and had gone back to get my tools and checklist. I was pulling off my racing suit when I heard the explosion."

"So, you didn't actually see it happen," Warren said.

"No. As soon as I heard the explosion, I turned to see what had happened. All I could see was black smoke and flames. I grabbed one of the fire extinguishers, jumped in my pickup truck and drove to the track. I was trying to put out the flames when the fire trucks pulled up."

Warren Reynolds faced the camera and said, "We have fire chief Wilson Barrett standing by here. Tell me, Chief, do you know what could have caused an explosion like that?"

A close-up of the fire chief's face showed up on the television screen—his name appeared at the bottom of the screen. "The matter is still under investigation," he said. "Kort told us that he was going to check something in the fuel system before the explosion occurred, so that's where we've started searching."

The next camera shot was of the wreckage. Warren Reynoldssaid, "With the big race less than 24 hours away, this is a real tragedy. I spoke with Chester Faraday, the owner of the Hollingsworth Oil car and his son Scott, who races the car."

The pretaped interview of Chester was shown. "My chief mechanic Kort Sinclair assured me the dragster was in good working order," Chester said. "I can't imagine what could have gone wrong. It's such a shock."

"Will you rebuild the car?" Warren asked.

"There's not much to rebuild. I'm not sure if we'll build another or not," Chester said.

Scott Faraday had also been taped earlier. Warren Reynolds asked him, "What's your reaction to all this?"

Scott looked down at the ground then lifted his head and gazed directly into the camera. "I'm sorry it all had to end this way," was all he said.

Warren Reynolds, live again, ended the report by saying, "The fire crew will continue their investigation into the cause of the explosion, and Channel 8 News will bring you updates as they occur. This is Warren Reynolds live at the Faraday test track in Gun Lake."

"Hey! They didn't even mention *me*," Johnnie said.

"I'm sure Kort didn't want you to get involved," Mrs. Jacobson said.

"But I *am* involved," Johnnie said. "I was there!"

Mrs. Jacobson had just opened her mouth to reply when the telephone rang. She picked up the receiver. "Hello? Yes, Danny, he's right here."

She handed the phone to Johnnie. "Hi, Danny. Yes, I just saw the news report. I know all about it," he said. "I was there when it happened."

Johnnie listened to his friend's excited voice on the other end of the line. Then he said, "Look, why don't you and the rest of the kids come over here after dinner. Let's meet in my backyard around 7 o'clock. Okay! Great! See you then."

He handed the receiver back to his mom but avoided looking at her. Finally, she knelt next to Johnnie, put her hand on his shoulder and said quietly, "You may have been there, Johnnie, but you *don't* know what happened. Don't let your imagination run wild."

Dinnertime at the Jacobson house was unusually

talkative that night. Johnnie told his family every-thing that happened. He was especially proud of the fact that he had been the one to call 9-1-1.

"Sounds like you handled yourself really well," Johnnie's father said. "In the midst of a very danger-ous accident, you were able to keep your cool and call for help. I'm impressed."

Johnnie beamed with pride. "So you think it was an accident?" Johnnie asked.

"Don't you?" Mr. Jacobson said.

"I—I guess so," Johnnie said. But in his heart he wasn't so sure.

At 7 o'clock, Danny, Katy and Travis arrived. Shortly after, Robyn knocked at the door, followed closely by Nick and Joey.

"Okay, Johnnie," Robyn said. "I hear you were at the test track when the car blew up. Is that *really* true?"

"Yes, it's *really* true," Johnnie said, mimicking her. He spent the next 30 minutes filling them in on all the details. Then he said, "My dad thinks it was an accident."

"Well, don't you think it was an accident?" Nick asked.

"I'm not so sure," Johnnie answered. "When Travis

and I were at the garage last week, we overheard Chester Faraday say maybe he just ought to blow up the car because it wasn't winning and Mr. Hollingsworth was threatening to not sponsor it anymore.

The kids looked at Travis to confirm what Johnnie had just said. "Yeah," Travis said, "I have to admit it, I was surprised to hear Mr. Faraday say that."

"And then," Johnnie continued, "I thought I saw Scott Faraday leave the garage. He must have heard Kort and Mr. Faraday talking about the fact that Scott wasn't a very good racer. Anyway, I went outside to find him—and I did. Scott admitted that he hated racing. As he was walking away toward the track, I heard him mutter under his breath something like, 'If I had a stick of dynamite I know what I'd blow up with it.'"

"Wow!" Danny said. "So we have *two* people who had good reason to blow up the car."

"Maybe Mr. Faraday told Kort to blow it up," Robyn suggested.

Everyone stopped talking and just stared at Robyn.

"Well, maybe not," Robyn said and shrugged her shoulders. "It was just a thought."

After everyone went home that evening, Johnnie

began thinking of all the pieces of evidence he had.

Hollingsworth was going to stop giving money to the Faradays if the car didn't start winning. Kort insisted the problem wasn't mechanical—yet it blew up.

Mr. Faraday was feeling desperate. He knew his son didn't like racing yet he had a lot of money sunk into the car, the garage, the pit crew and the test track. He could get a lot of insurance money now that the car was destroyed.

Scott Faraday openly didn't like racing but was doing it to please his father. With the car destroyed, he could go on writing songs.

And what if Robyn was right? What if Mr. Faraday had hired Kort to blow up the car? Kort certainly had every opportunity to do it.

It was all too much for Johnnie to think about. Regardless of what had happened, Johnnie knew there was another Gun Lake mystery to solve—and he knew that the Gun Lake kids were going to get involved once again.

CHAPTER FIVE

The Day of the Race

"Someone's chasing me!" Johnnie yelled. He tried to escape. His breath came in hard, short gasps. Though he pushed with all his might, his wheelchair would not move. "Gotta make it to the alley," he gasped.

Suddenly, a loud explosion thundered behind him. Johnnie looked back only to see a wall of flames moving directly toward him. The heat was suffocating. "Get me out of here!" he yelled.

Johnnie awoke with a start. His bedcovers were wrapped around his neck and arms, and he was sweating. Quickly, he untangled himself and glanced at the clock. "Only 3:00 AM," he groaned.

Johnnie laid on his back and stared toward the ceiling. The danger he had experienced in his dream left him feeling shaky.

"Johnnie?" His mother whispered through his open bedroom door. "Are you okay?"

"Yeah, Mom," Johnnie answered softly. "I just had

a bad dream, that's all."

"Want to talk about it? Sometimes it helps to tell someone about a bad dream."

Johnnie briefly explained the dream. Then, unexpectedly, he began to cry. "I can't believe the Faradays' car is gone," he sobbed. "We were going to go to the big race and everything, but now—"

Mrs. Jacobson hugged her son. "I know you're disappointed, Johnnie. We were *all* looking forward to going to the race. But what's done is done."

"It's not just the race," Johnnie said. "I'm wondering who blew up that car."

"Who said someone blew it up?" Mrs. Jacobson asked.

"No one—yet. But I have this feeling that someone did." By the night light in his room he could see his mom's worried face. "I'll be okay now, Mom. I think I can get back to sleep."

Mrs. Jacobson kissed Johnnie on the forehead. "All right," she said. "If you need me, I'm just down the hall."

After she left, Johnnie's tears began again. Try as he might, he could not dismiss the feeling he had.

Seeds of doubt had been planted in Johnnie's mind about Kort. He struggled to keep them from growing. "No!" he blurted. "Kort did *not* blow up that car. Why would he bring me to the track if he knew he was going to do that?" Satisfied for the moment, Johnnie rolled over and slept.

"Beep! Beep! Beep! Beep!" The persistent sound awakened Johnnie. Sleepily he turned over and pressed the button on top of his alarm clock radio. It was 7:30 in the morning. He was about to roll over and go back to sleep when his mom came into the room.

"Johnnie, it's time to get up," she said. "We have to get ready for the race."

Johnnie stared at his mother, not believing what he was hearing. "We're still going to the race? Even after what happened?"

"Yes. Mr. Faraday called earlier this morning and insisted we be there as his guests. He, Scott and Kort will be there. He said he'd really like to have us and all the families there."

"Cool!" Johnnie said.

All thoughts of last night's nightmare and his doubts about Kort disappeared as he got dressed and ate breakfast. He pulled out the special passes Mr. Faraday had given them a few weeks ago. They were going to have some of the best seats in the whole place.

By the time the Jacobsons arrived at the track, Danny, Katy, Joey and Nick were already there. It wasn't long before Robyn and Travis showed up with their families. They were greeted by Scott Faraday himself.

"Come on over to our booth," he said. "You'll have a great view of everything."

Scott asked if he could help Johnnie up the steep ramp that led to their seats. "Before I take you up there, Johnnie," Scott began, "I just want to let you know that I really *do* feel badly that the car blew up."

"I thought you'd be *glad*," Johnnie said. "At least you won't have to race anymore."

"Well, I have to admit, I am glad about that part of it," Scott said. "But I feel badly for my dad. He says he's not going to build another dragster. I just don't know how that's going to affect him. Racing was everything to him—and though he has lots of other things to do, I think he's going to miss being in the middle of all the activity at the racetrack."

Johnnie looked up at Scott and smiled. "Well he can still race *me* if he wants to!"

Scott laughed. "I'm sure he'll enjoy that!"

Up in the stands, Johnnie took a seat next to his father. Johnnie looked around and spotted Mr. Faraday sitting at the far end of the spectator booth. Johnnie searched the rest of the booth but couldn't find Kort.

"I wonder where Kort is?" Johnnie said to his dad.

Mr. Jacobson scanned the booth and the general

area. "I'm sure he's around somewhere," he said. "He might be running a little late."

"I've never known Kort to be late for *anything*," Johnnie said.

While waiting for his friend to arrive, Johnnie decided to enjoy looking around. Behind him, the stands were packed with people dressed in colorful T-shirts and shorts. Vendors were already out selling drinks, hot dogs and bags of chips and peanuts to the anxiously awaiting fans.

Along the walls of the track, colorful advertising was painted for each of the sponsors. Cameramen, newsmen and track officials scrambled around making the final preparations before the races began.

The black asphalt of the two parallel tracks was in perfect condition. Dragsters would race two at a time down the quarter-mile track—each in its own lane. The lanes were separated from each other by a wide, painted strip. An electronic timing device would automatically record each car's time and speed.

Already, Johnnie could see the first two dragsters being positioned at the starting line. Johnnie turned to look behind him again. Where was Kort?

Just then, Johnnie noticed a police officer walking toward their booth. That wasn't totally unusual, as police officers were on hand to help control the crowds. Other emergency workers were at the track too—just in case. But when the officer came up into the booth and began talking to Mr. Faraday, Johnnie's heart began beating faster.

Johnnie saw Scott join the conversation. The officer said something and Scott's mouth dropped open in surprise. Mr. Faraday nodded and said something, then maneuvered his chair around so he could go down the ramp with the policeman.

Scott sat, slumped slightly in his chair, and stared straight ahead. "I'd better go over and find out what's going on," Mr. Jacobson said.

"Can I go too?" Johnnie asked.

"No, you stay here." Mr. Jacobson read the disappointed look in his son's face. "I promise I'll tell you everything I find out."

Johnnie saw Danny and Katy's father go over to Scott too. The other families watched Scott from their seats. Johnnie figured they would just wait—like he was—for news of what was going on.

After what seemed to be a very long time, Mr. Jacobson returned to his seat. His face was grim. Robyn and her parents came over to where the Jacobsons were seated.

"What is it?" Mr. Anderson asked.

"Bad news, I'm afraid. It seems the investigators

found some bomb making materials in the Faradays' garage. They were hidden in Kort's tool chest. The fire chief confirmed that the car was blown up. I'm afraid Kort's been arrested."

"No!" Johnnie cried. "He couldn't have done it!"

"Why do you say that?" his father asked. "Have you remembered something about what happened that would help Kort?"

Johnnie looked at his father. Then he looked at Robyn and her parents. He wanted to say, "Yes! I know who did it. I saw everything." But he couldn't say that because it wasn't true.

"But why would he do it?" Johnnie asked miserably.

"I'm not saying that he *did* do it," Mr. Jacobson said. Scott did tell me that Mr. Faraday had recently made Kort a partner with him. As partner, Kort had invested some of his own money in the car. The police are wondering if Kort blew up the car in order to collect the insurance money."

"The insurance money?" Robyn asked. "Why would he want insurance money if he could make more money winning races?"

"Well," said Mr. Anderson, "that's probably the point. They *weren't* winning any races. In fact, they were probably losing money."

"Kort wouldn't care about the money," Johnnie cried. "He's just not that kind of person."

"Son, everyone needs money," Mr. Jacobson said.

"Well, he's making money selling and fixing wheelchairs," Johnnie said. He turned away, not wanting to discuss it further. Those seeds of doubt had begun to sprout—and Johnnie hated it.

Throughout the rest of the afternoon, Johnnie's thoughts were far from the racetrack.

Kort wouldn't have done it, Johnnie reasoned with himself. *Or would he?*

CHAPTER SIX

More Evidence

"Johnnie, my brother and his friend will take us to the Faradays garage this afternoon," Robyn said over the phone.

"How are we going to get past the security gate?" Johnnie asked. "I sure don't know the code."

Robyn answered, "My brother Josh helps take care of the grounds out there. He has to mow the lawn and do some other stuff. His friend Tom works out there too during the summer. They said there's enough room in the van for the two of them and five kids to come along, if we want. So I thought you and I would go along with Danny, Katy and Travis."

"Are the police still investigating out there?" Johnnie asked.

"As far as I know, the investigation is done. Josh just warned me to stay out of the way. But while we're there—staying out of the way, of course—we can just sort of look around," she said.

"Hmmm," said Johnnie. "Another Gun Lake adventure?"

"Exactly! Let's look for clues."

The idea of another mystery to solve gave Johnnie new hope of somehow clearing Kort from any suspicion. If there was something out there to find, the Gun Lake kids would find it.

Shortly after lunch, Josh and Tom pulled up in the Jacobsons' driveway. Mrs. Jacobson wasn't too sure she wanted Johnnie to be out at the test track. But the look of excitement on her son's face—something that had not been there since he had learned of Kort's arrest— made her finally give in.

After assuring his mom at least a dozen times that he would be careful, he and his friends were on their way. Travis pulled out an old magnifying glass and a plastic sandwich bag.

"What's that stuff for?" Katy asked.

"This isn't *stuff*," Travis said. "These are tools we can use in our investigation. If we're looking for materials to make bombs out of—like powder, fuses and wires— then we're going to need a magnifying glass. And we'll need something to put our evidence in," he added swinging the plastic bag in front of Katy's face.

Katy rolled her eyes. "Whatever," she said.

Danny said, "I thought the investigators already found bomb supplies in Kort's tool chest."

"Obviously, someone planted those things there," Travis said. "That someone may have neglected to put all the bomb materials in Kort's tool chest."

"You seem pretty sure that Kort didn't do it," Danny remarked.

"Of course I'm sure. I've known Kort a long time, and I know he would never do anything like that," Travis said. "Right, Johnnie?"

Johnnie's stomach was beginning to get tight. He wanted to believe Kort wasn't involved. It would be fantastic if there were another person involved. But Johnnie knew that it was only Kort and himself at the track the day the dragster blew up.

"Well, Johnnie?" Travis demanded. "Do you think Kort did it?"

"I—I'm not sure," Johnnie said. He avoided looking at Travis or the other kids. He felt like he was betraying one of his best friends.

"I don't believe it!" Travis yelled. "Kort has gone out of his way to be nice to you. He invited *you*—not any of the rest of us—to watch him test drive that dragster. Didn't you tell me that he even taught you some strategy for playing laser tag? Does that sound like the kind of person who would go around blowing up cars?"

"Hey, take it easy, Travis," Danny said. "No one *wants* to believe Kort is guilty. That's why we're going out to the test track today—to look for clues. If we can find something that would prove someone else blew up the car, then we can prove Kort is innocent."

Travis turned his back on the group and spent the rest of the ride glaring out the side window. Johnnie, who was seated in the captain's seat nearest the side door, fought back tears. Was he a traitor for suspecting Kort? No, he told himself. *I'm going to go out there and find something that will prove—once and for all—that Kort is innocent.*

At the gate, Josh punched in the code numbers and waited for the heavy gate to open. Once inside, he drove the long, blue van to the maintenance shed.

"Okay, you guys," Josh said, as he unloaded Johnnie's wheelchair, "just stay out of trouble. Tom and I are going to use the riding lawnmowers. We'll start over there," he said, pointing at the field opposite where they were standing, "and work our way back here."

"How long do you think we'll be here?" Robyn asked.

"It will probably take us three hours to mow down all the weeds near the track," Josh answered.

"We brought a cooler full of pop that we'll leave in the van. If you get thirsty, help yourselves.

"My mom also packed a bunch of cookies," Tom added. "Help yourselves to those but just remember— there's *seven* of us." He pointed to himself and Josh for emphasis.

Josh and Tom took off toward the shed while the other kids decided where to look first.

"Let's see," said Travis. "It's about an eighth of a mile from the garage to the beginning of the track. And the track is a little over a quarter of a mile long."

"Your point being," said Robyn.

"I'm going over the facts," Travis said. "Johnnie said Kort walked back to the beginning of the track to let him know he was going to get some tools. Kort then took the tow truck back to the garage. Johnnie, about how long was Kort gone before you heard the explosion?"

Johnnie thought for a moment. "I'd say he was gone no longer than five minutes. But I couldn't say for sure."

"And then the next time you saw Kort, he was driving the pickup truck to the dragster, right?" Danny asked.

"Right," Johnnie said.

"So, he *could* have gone back to the garage and

detonated the bomb," Robyn said.

"Well—it's *possible*," Johnnie replied.

"But it's also possible that someone else detonated the bomb," Travis insisted.

"I honestly don't remember anyone else being here," Johnnie said. "When we got to the track, there wasn't a person in sight."

"What exactly are we doing here?" Katy said. "What are we looking for that the police haven't already found?"

"I just have a gut feeling that there's something out here the police have overlooked. And I don't think it's in the garage. Let's just say that Kort is innocent. If he *didn't* detonate the bomb, then whoever did wouldn't be in the garage. He'd be somewhere outside where he would have a good view of both the track and the garage," Travis said. He looked around the grounds. "The only place he could have hidden was in those woods." He pointed to a group of trees about 100 yards away from the track. They grew parallel to the track and stopped about 25 feet from the driveway leading to the garage.

"I guess we search the woods then," Danny said.

"Let's grab some cookies and pop and head on out," said Johnnie. He wasn't sure what they would find or even if they did find something that it would clear Kort, but he was beginning to get caught up in the adventure.

When they reached the woods, Robyn noticed that there was no path. "You're not going to be able to push your chair in there," she said.

"Well, I'm *not* going to be left behind!" Johnnie said.

"No one said you're going to be left behind," Robyn said. "We'll just need to push you, that's all."

"Hey, look!" Travis said. He was already about 25 feet into woods. "There are some broken branches and trampled brush. Looks like someone or some big animal came through here recently."

When the rest of the kids caught up to Travis, they saw a rough path zig-zagging through the trees and bushes.

"Let's follow it," Katy said. Travis led the way with Katy and Robyn close behind him. Danny and Johnnie followed behind, keeping a careful lookout.

Streams of light filtered through the tall, thin trees making it easy to follow the path. After winding their way for about ten minutes, the path suddenly stopped.

When they looked out toward the track, they were amazed to find themselves within clear view of the place where the dragster had blown up.

"Okay, everybody," Travis said. "Let's focus our search right around here."

"So we're looking for powder, string, fuses and what else?" Katy asked.

"We're looking for *anything* that doesn't look like it grew here," said Travis.

"Johnnie, stay here and watch to make sure no one sees us," Danny said.

Johnnie felt angry. He wanted to crawl around the path with the rest of the kids. He hated being left behind. It was times like this that Johnnie struggled the most with his disability.

"Stupid wheelchair," Johnnie muttered. "My legs are totally *useless*!" he shouted.

Danny, who was about 20 feet away, turned and looked at his friend. "Did you say something?" he yelled.

"Um, I just said I hope you... don't turn up *clueless*."

"Oh! Right!" Danny said. He looked puzzled but turned and began walking down the path again.

Johnnie chuckled. "Useless—clueless! That was pretty good!" he said. He watched while his friends searched along the path. "I guess being a lookout isn't so bad," he said. "In fact, it's probably the most dangerous part of this whole mission. What if they do find something? And what if the person who triggered the bomb discovers it's missing and comes back to look for it?" A shiver of excitement trickled down Johnnie's spine.

He scanned the horizon, looking for anything unusual. Most of the time, he anxiously watched his friends scurrying around on hands and knees.

"Hey! I found something," Robyn said, as she walked over to where Johnnie sat waiting.

She stood, holding something small and white in her hand. The others ran over to where she was.

"What is it?" Danny asked.

Robyn showed them a wadded up piece of paper. "It looks like someone put their chewing gum inside a piece of paper." she said. "Not much of a clue."

She was about to throw it back onto the ground when Travis snatched it from her fingers.

"In the investigation game, *everything* unusual is a clue," he said. "And finding a piece of paper with gum in it is unusual. This is private land. We know that someone has been here recently. In fact, the trail ends conveniently across from the place where the dragster blew up. And you just happen to find this paper and gum right here. I'd say it's a very important clue."

"Open the paper," Johnnie said. "It looks like there's writing on it."

The side with the gum in it was blank, but sure enough, on the outside there were some words and part of a drawing of some sort. It read:

GER
DATION
skin exposure
attered radiation
Laser Product

"I wonder what the other half of the message says," Danny said.

While the other kids chattered about the possibilities, Johnnie stared at the word, "Laser."

There was only one person he knew of who was an expert in lasers.

CHAPTER SEVEN

The Stranger

"Robyn!" Josh yelled. "Come on, we're ready to go."

Robyn and the other kids were slowly making their way back out of the woods toward the road. Robyn had managed to unstick the gum from the inside of the paper she found. She then carefully folded the paper and put it in her pocket.

"We're coming!" she yelled out. Everyone continued to guess what the paper might mean— everyone but Johnnie. He remained silent—lost in his own unsettled thoughts.

When they reached the maintenance shed, Josh and Tom were waiting for them. "What were you guys doing in the woods?" Josh asked.

"We were exploring," Robyn explained.

"Well, let's get you guys home," said Josh. "Tom and I have plans for tonight. We're going to see that movie, *The Weapon*, that's showing at the Gun Lake Cinema."

"Yeah," said Tom. "I hear it's got some really awesome

lasers in it."

Once safely secured in the van, Johnnie leaned back in his seat and stared out the van's side window. In low voices, the other kids continued to talk about the clue they had found. Johnnie remained silent, purposely tuning out his friends' conversation.

Over and over, in his mind's eye, Johnnie could see the word, "Laser." He tried not to think about it but the picture of that word pulled his thoughts like a magnet.

"Hey, Johnnie! You're awful quiet," Danny said. The sound of his name made Johnnie snap out of his daze. "What are you thinking about?"

Johnnie studied his friend for a moment. Ever since Johnnie and his family had moved to Gun Lake, Danny had been his closest friend. Of all the Gun Lake kids, Danny was the one Johnnie felt most comfortable with. He knew he could talk to Danny about anything. But as much as he wanted to, in some ways Johnnie didn't feel ready to tell Danny about his growing suspicions about Kort.

"I-I guess I'm just tired," Johnnie finally answered. The truth was, Johnnie *did* feel tired, though he hadn't done much physically. His feelings of anger, fear and suspicion were fighting with the admiration and deep respect Johnnie felt for Kort. The whole thing made Johnnie want to take a long nap. *Maybe when I wake up, it will all be over*, Johnnie thought.

That evening, Johnnie was unusually quiet at dinnertime. He helped his mother clear the dinner table and then wheeled himself out to the family room to watch television.

"Want to talk about it?" Mr. Jacobson asked. His voice startled Johnnie.

"What makes you think there's something to talk about?" Johnnie said.

"Well, either something is on your mind, or you've suddenly taken a big interest in lipstick commercials."

Johnnie suddenly realized he had been staring at the television not really seeing what was on the screen. He laughed. "I guess I *do* have something on my mind."

Johnnie took a big breath and then blurted out all his fears and suspicions. "I know I'm not supposed to jump to conclusions," he said, "but Kort is the only person I know of who knows a lot about lasers. He even once told me that he had worked on secret military lasers."

Johnnie's father frowned. "I have to admit, it doesn't look good for Kort. You know, we really should go to the police with the information you just shared with me."

Johnnie leaned forward and grabbed his dad's

hand. "No! I mean, let's wait a few days—*please!"*

"Okay, Johnnie. We'll see what happens in the next few days. But—and listen carefully—if something doesn't happen that will clear Kort, we're going to have to tell the police. Understood?"

Johnnie nodded his head. Inside he felt both relieved and worried.

* * * *

Late the next morning, Johnnie was awakened by a phone call from Danny. "Hey! Guess what? Kort's got a lawyer," Danny said.

"Well, of course he does," Johnnie said. He felt irritated at having been awakened with such obvious news.

"No, you don't understand," Danny insisted. "He's not just any lawyer. He's a friend of Kort's from the Vietnam War. They served together."

"How in the world did he know Kort needed a lawyer?" Johnnie asked, now fully awake.

"He said he saw a newspaper story about it," Danny answered. "Anyway, he's down at the jail, talking with Kort now."

"How do you know all of this?" Johnnie asked.

"My dad was visiting Kort this morning, when Kort got the message that he had another visitor. When he asked who it was, the guard said it was a

Nathaniel Owens and that he wanted to be Kort's lawyer. My dad left so the two of them could talk."

"Did your dad see this Nathaniel Owens?" Johnnie asked.

"Yeah, he was waiting in the lobby. My dad said he was big, carried a black briefcase and wore army fatigues," Danny said.

"Army fatigues!" Johnnie was surprised. "I thought lawyers were supposed to wear suits."

Johnnie and his friends decided to meet at the Lakeside Ice Cream Shop—for two reasons. First, they had the best milkshakes in town and second, the store was located across the street from the Gun Lake Police Department, where Kort was being held.

News of the stranger in town was buzzing around Gun Lake. As far as anyone knew, Nathaniel Owens was still in the jail talking to Kort.

"Look! There he is!" Joey yelled.

Scampering for a spot at the window, all the customers in the ice cream shop—including the Gun Lake kids—craned their necks to get a view of the tall man in the army fatigues.

As Mr. Owens walked down the street, Johnnie thought he detected a slight limp.

"Let's follow him," Johnnie said.

CHAPTER EIGHT

The Other Half of the Clue

One by one the kids tumbled out of the Lakeside Ice Cream shop. "Try to look casual," Travis said. He took the lead, followed closely by Danny and Johnnie. Joey and Nick paired off and trailed the older boys by a couple feet. Robyn and Katy decided to walk on the other side of the street.

Mr. Owens was easy to spot. His army fatigues stood out against the sidewalk and pavement. He walked at a steady pace, never once turning around. When he reached the Shoreline Motel, he entered the door to the lobby.

"Besides working at the racetrack, my brother works part-time for the Shoreline Motel," Robyn said. "Maybe he could find out some information for us."

"Good!" said Travis. "You follow up on that and, in the meantime, I'll go visit Kort and see what I can find out from him."

"Johnnie, why don't you go with Travis?" Katy said. "After all, you were the one who was there when the car blew up."

"I-I don't know," Johnnie said. "Maybe just one of us visiting would be enough."

"You know, Kort's been asking about you," Danny said. "He wonders why you haven't been down to see him yet. I think it would mean a lot to him if you would go."

"I don't know what I'd say," Johnnie said. "Besides, I think my mom wants me to help her around the house today."

"Yeah, right!" Travis said. "That's about the lamest excuse I've ever heard."

"Oh, great! *Now* you're making 'lame' jokes," Johnnie said. He smiled weakly.

Travis just frowned. "How can you doubt some-one like Kort?" Travis demanded. "You trust him with fixing your wheelchair. You trusted him enough to go with him to the track that day. He's always doing nice things for you. What makes you suspect him now?" Travis was shouting now.

Johnnie wanted to tell them about Kort's knowledge of lasers. He wanted to let them all know that Kort had done some secret military work that involved lasers. He wanted to grab that piece of paper from Robyn and wave it in their faces, pointing out the word "laser" and then asking *them* what their conclusions would be. But he couldn't. He didn't want to believe that his friend was guilty. He was hoping that somehow Mr. Owens would discover the truth and that Kort would be let out of jail.

Travis' shouting was followed by complete silence. Johnnie stared at the ground while his friends stared at both him and Travis.

Finally, Danny spoke. "Look, no one knows what happened. Let's hope this Mr. Owens can help get to the bottom of this. Johnnie, if you don't want to visit Kort right now, then that's okay. Why don't you come over to my house with Joey, Nick, Katy and me. When Travis and Robyn get their information, they can come over and tell us what they found out."

"Well, okay," Johnnie said. He looked up at Travis, who still looked angry. "I really do *want* to believe Kort is innocent. Tell him I'll come to see him tomorrow."

"Look, if you want Kort to know you're coming to see him, then *you* tell him," Travis said. Then he turned and walked back toward the police station.

*   *   *   *

It was late in the afternoon before Travis and Robyn showed up at Danny's house.

"Travis, you go first," Robyn said. "What did Kort

have to say about Nathaniel Owens?"

"Well," Travis began, "Kort was as surprised to see him as we were. Mr. Owens was a staff sergeant in the army. During the Vietnam War, he and Kort were in Cambodia trying to secure an airstrip in a town called Snoul.

"Kort said they knew the enemy was close by. But they needed that airstrip so supply planes could fly in and out.

"He said that Snoul had lots of rubber plantations, and one of the largest ones was along the road to the airstrip. Someone tipped off the Americans that the enemy was hiding among the rows and rows of rubber trees, waiting to ambush them.

"One of the soldiers started yelling, 'I've got one!' So Kort, Owens and two other guys ran over to a bunker, where this enemy guy was hiding."

"What's a 'bunker'?" Joey asked.

"It's an underground bomb shelter," Johnnie said.

"Anyway," Travis continued, "they are trying to dig this guy out when suddenly he throws a homemade grenade at them. It lands near Kort. Owens sees it and dives at Kort, knocking him out of the way. When the grenade blew up, Kort was knocked unconscious."

"What happened to Owens?" Katy asked.

"His leg was messed up pretty badly," Travis said.

"Eventually, he had to have it amputated below the knee."

"You mean they cut off his leg?" Nick asked. "Well then how can he walk? We saw him walking on *two* legs."

"Yeah, how can he walk?" Joey chimed in.

"He has a *prosthesis*," Johnnie said.

"A pro—what?" Nick asked.

"A prosthesis—an artificial limb. In this case, an artificial leg."

"Whoa! Cool!" Nick said. "I bet it looks just like that pirate's wooden leg. What's his name?"

"I think you're referring to Blackbeard," Katy said. "He had a leg that looked like an upside-down baseball bat."

"No," Johnnie said with a laugh, "the artificial legs they have now are much different. They're much more real looking and, with lots of practice, some people with artificial legs can run and even jump hurdles."

"Wow! That would be awesome," Joey said.

"But getting back to Owens, what happened after he lost his leg?" Johnnie asked.

"Kort said he was returned to active duty. He was hoping to be promoted but was passed over, even though he received a medal for bravery. Kort eventually was promoted to the rank of lieutenant but lost track of Owens. That's why Kort was so surprised when Owens showed up. Kort said that Owens told him he went to law school after he got out the army."

"So is Kort going to use him as his attorney?" Robyn asked.

"Kort said Owens offered to be his lawyer at no charge—as a favor to an 'old army buddy,' as he put it," Travis said. "But Kort isn't sure he wants Nathaniel Owens as an attorney. This is really weird."

"It sure is," Robyn said. "And so is that piece of paper we found. I showed it to my brother who is really into weapons and the latest technology. He said it looked familiar—especially the words 'Laser Product.'

"He said that he and Tom bought a book about how to make your own laser gun."

"No way," Johnnie said. "There can't be a book about making laser guns. That's supposed to be a top military secret."

"I didn't believe it at first, either," Robyn said. "Then Josh showed me the book! It's called, *Build Your Own Laser, Phaser, Ion Ray Gun and Other Working Space-Age Projects* by Robert E. Iannini. It was published in 1983. In it were instructions on how to build a laser gun!"

"Let's get a copy of that book!" Joey said.

"Believe me, it's all very technical. It has to do with magnets, electrodes, ions—all sorts of stuff I don't even know the meaning of," Robyn said. "But one thing that caught Josh's eye that he wanted me to see was a label that is supposed to be attached to a laser weapon like the one they showed in the book."

She reached inside her pocket and brought out the torn piece of paper. Then she showed them another piece of paper.

"I think we have the other half of the clue," she said with a smile on her face. "According to this book, the label should look like this."

DANGER
LASER RADIATION
Avoid eye or skin exposure
to direct or scattered radiation.
Class IV Laser Product

"What we have in our hands is the right half of a label that someone was supposed to have put on the laser gun," Travis said.

"Kort *could* have done it," Johnnie blurted. "He told me he had worked with the military in making laser weapons."

The others looked at Johnnie in disbelief. "Are you sure?" Danny asked.

"Yes, I'm sure. He told me himself!" Johnnie felt

frustrated. "And I told my dad the same thing last night, and he wants us to tell the police."

"Oh, no!" Katy cried. "We can't tell the police. We've got to keep looking for clues."

"Well, I don't know how much of a clue this is," Robyn said. "But Josh found out that Mr. Owens has been in town since before the explosion. He's been staying at the motel for the last two weeks!"

"That's really strange," Travis said. "He told Kort he had come here after reading about the explosion in a newspaper."

Johnnie felt a surge of new hope. Maybe—just maybe—Mr. Owens held the key that would unlock this whole mystery and set Kort free.

CHAPTER NINE

A Break in the Case— And a Fire!

"I could lose my job, if I get caught," Josh said. "I'm not part of housekeeping. I can't just go into someone's motel room and look around."

"But you *won't* get caught," Robyn pleaded. "We'll keep a lookout for anyone coming down the hall."

"It's for Kort," Travis added. "Maybe there is evidence in Mr. Owens' room that could get Kort out of jail."

Johnnie watched Josh pace back and forth across the Anderson's living room floor. He stopped, gazed out the window and then started pacing again.

"I know it's for a good cause," Josh said slowly. "I *could* probably get away with it too. But it's not right. I felt uncomfortable just finding out how long Mr. Owens has been registered at the motel."

He looked at the disappointed looks on the faces of his sister's friends and added, "Tell you what. If, for some reason, I am asked to go into Mr. Owens' room—

on official business—then I'll take a look around."

"That sounds fair," Johnnie said. "What would make your visit to his room 'official'?"

"I'm part of maintenance, so I get to fix broken toilets, stopped up drains, air conditioners that don't work—you know, stuff like that," Josh answered.

Johnnie sighed. "Fat chance of any of that stuff breaking down," he said.

"Well, I don't want you to get your hopes up," Josh answered. "But I'll keep my eyes and ears open. I really *do* want to help Kort. I just don't want to do something that isn't right."

Johnnie took a quick look at his watch. "I have to go," he said. "My dad and I are going to visit Kort this afternoon, and I have to go get ready."

"So you're *really* going through with it," Travis said. "I really thought you'd chicken out."

Johnnie resisted making a sarcastic remark. Instead, he said, "Josh isn't the *only* person who can do what is right. I said I would visit Kort today, and I will."

* * * *

Johnnie and his father were escorted to the sixth floor of the police station, where the jail was located.

"Gee, this looks like something out of the movies," Johnnie said as he looked around. The guard unlocked a door that led into a narrow visiting area to let them in. There were six booths, separated from each other by a dull green metal partition. Each booth contained a chair and a telephone. The visitor was supposed to sit in the chair, look through the non-breakable plexiglass window and use the telephone to talk with the prisoner.

There was just enough room for Johnnie's wheelchair to make it through the door and down the aisle. The guard removed one of the chairs from the booth nearest the door so Johnnie could position his wheelchair in front of the window.

Johnnie and his dad waited for about five minutes before they saw a guard open a heavy metal door leading from the jail to the prisoner side of the visiting area. Johnnie saw Kort walk in. He was wearing the normal "jail uniform" of blue jeans and a gray-blue shirt. "Property of Gun Lake City Jail" was stamped in black letters over the front, left pocket of the shirt.

Johnnie blinked back tears when he saw Kort's smiling face. Nervously, Johnnie picked up the telephone and watched as Kort picked up the telephone on his side of the booth.

"I am *so* glad to see you, Johnnie," Kort said. "I've

been wondering when you'd come around."

Johnnie could feel his throat tighten up. He knew that tears were collecting in his eyes, and he felt angry with himself that he couldn't do more to control his emotions. Unable to hold the tears any longer, Johnnie put his head down and began to sob. He felt his father's reassuring hand gently pat his shoulders.

Mr. Jacobson gently took the phone from Johnnie and said to Kort, "This has been very hard on him. Your friendship means a lot to him."

Suddenly, Johnnie grabbed the phone away from his dad. "That's *not* why I'm crying," he stammered. "Kort, I have to be honest with you. I stayed away because I was convinced that you had actually done it. When the other kids and I went out to the track with Josh and Tom, we found a piece of paper that had the word 'laser' written on it. It was in the woods, right across from where the dragster had been when it blew up."

Johnnie went on to tell both Kort and his father about how they found out what was on the other half of that piece of paper.

"I just knew it was you," Johnnie said. "But I didn't want to believe it."

Kort lowered his head and sighed. "Johnnie, you said earlier that you *were* convinced I was guilty. Does that mean you're *not* convinced now?"

Johnnie looked straight into Kort's eyes. "I'm *not* convinced at all—and let me tell you why."

Kort and Mr. Jacobson were fascinated when Johnnie told them about Mr. Owens' two-week stay at the Shoreline Motel.

"I can't imagine why he would be here in the first place," Kort said, shaking his head. "It doesn't make sense."

"No, it certainly doesn't," Mr. Jacobson agreed. "Have you told your attorney about Mr. Owens?"

"I mentioned that an old army friend of mine had become an attorney and had offered to represent me," Kort said.

"I think it's time you tell your attorney about the clue *and* the history behind Mr. Owens—including the fact that he has been here since before the dragster blew up," Mr. Jacobson said.

"And Johnnie," Mr. Jacobson continued, "I'm afraid you and the kids are going to have to turn that piece of paper over to the police. We cannot obstruct the law by withholding potential evidence. Agreed?"

"Agreed," Johnnie said. Then to Kort he said, "I'm really sorry I doubted you. I guess I jumped to conclusions."

"I can see why you'd come to some of the conclusions that you did," Kort said. Then he smiled and put his hand on the glass. "Give me five," he said.

Johnnie put the phone back on the desk, then quickly picked it up again. "Hey!" he said. "What about Mr. Faraday or Scott? Maybe Mr. Faraday hired Mr. Owens to blow up the car so he could collect the insurance. Or maybe Scott hired Mr. Owens to blow up the car so he wouldn't have to race anymore!"

"Or maybe," Kort interrupted, "Mr. Owens *didn't* blow up the car. Aren't you jumping to conclusions again?"

Johnnie grinned. "Yeah, I guess. But I heard that you might have blown it up because you wanted the insurance money. So, I'm just saying both Mr. Faraday and Scott had reasons to blow it up too."

Kort shook his head and smiled at Johnnie.

"You have a point there, Johnnie. You definitely have a *good* point."

Before Johnnie and his dad left the police station, they told Police Chief Brian Davis about the clue and about Mr. Owens. "Robyn Anderson has the piece of paper," Johnnie said. "Do you want me to have her bring it to you?"

"That's would be fine, Johnnie," Chief Davis said. "We'll take it from here. And thank you for bringing this evidence to our attention."

That evening, Mrs. Jacobson called Johnnie and his dad into the living room. "Warren Reynolds of TV8 just announced there was a break in Kort's case. He said details would follow the commercial."

The Jacobsons' eyes were riveted to the television through the next four commercials. Finally the news came back on. Mr. Reynolds, sitting behind the news desk, looked into the camera and said, "New evidence recently turned into the Gun Lake Police Department has stepped up the investigation of the apparent bombing of the Hollingsworth Oil dragster.

"The dragster, owned by Chester Faraday, was destroyed on July 28 at the Faraday test strip."

A picture of the demolished dragster flashed up on the television screen. "According to Gun Lake's police chief Brian Davis, an unidentified source provided information that indicates the dragster may have been blown up through use of laser technology.

"Police arrested Kort Sinclair, long-time chief mechanic for the Faradays, on July 29, after bomb-making materials were found in his possession. This is what the police chief had to say about the new evidence . . ."

A video-taped interview between a newsperson and Chief Davis was aired. Chief Davis said, "We're confident that we're getting closer to the truth. We now believe we know *how* the bomb was set off but we're unsure as to who may have done it."

The reporter asked, "Does that mean you may have another suspect in the bombing?"

"We're checking all possibilities," was all the police chief would say.

Warren Reynolds came back on the screen and concluded the story by saying, "We'll keep you updated as new evidence comes to light."

Mrs. Jacobson turned off the television. "Well!" she said. "Sounds like the clue you gave may be helpful to Kort after all. I heard that Chester Faraday may pay his bail and that he might be getting out of jail tomorrow."

"Pay his bail?" Johnnie asked. "What does that mean?"

"Bail is the amount of money the judge says must

be paid in order for a prisoner to get out of jail. Just because he's not behind bars doesn't mean he's free, however," Mr. Jacobson said. "It means he can wait for his trial at home."

"What if he runs away?" Johnnie said.

"The person who paid the bail would lose all the money," Mr. Jacobson said. "If, however, he shows up for his trial, the person would get most of the money back. Part of the money would go to the company that holds the bail money."

"Why do you think Mr. Faraday is willing to pay Kort's bail now?" Johnnie asked. "Why didn't he do it before?"

"Perhaps Mr. Faraday wasn't sure he could trust Kort," Mrs. Jacobson suggested. "After all, he just lost a very expensive car, and the evidence pointed to Kort, at the time."

"Well, that piece of paper *still* points to him," Johnnie said.

"Yes, but the fact that this mysterious Nathaniel Owens has been in town since before the explosion, takes some of the suspicion off of Kort," Mr. Jacobson said.

That night Johnnie could hardly get to sleep. Why would Mr. Owens come to town in the first place?

Why would he suddenly show up in Kort's life after all these years? Since Mr. Owens had been in the army, was it possible *he* had some knowledge of lasers?

The questions turned in Johnnie's mind like an endless merry-go-round. He drifted off to a troubled sleep.

He awoke early the next morning. It was a hot and humid Saturday. He could hear his mother and father talking in the kitchen. Their voices were low, so he couldn't quite make out what they said. Then he heard his father say Kort's name. Curiosity welled up inside of him as Johnnie sat up in bed and reached for his wheelchair. Making sure the brake was set, he transferred into his chair.

"Good morning, everyone," Johnnie called out as he rolled into the kitchen.

"Well! Good morning to *you!*" his mother said, surprised. "What brings you out of bed so early?"

"I thought I heard you two talking about Kort," Johnnie answered. He plopped two pieces of bread in the toaster and then proceeded to pour himself a large glass of orange juice.

His dad chuckled. "You don't miss much, do you? Yes, as a matter of fact, we got a phone call from Mr. Faraday last night, after you had gone to bed. He confirmed that he was paying Kort's bail. Kort's attorney is going to pick him up at the jail and take him home this afternoon."

"Yes!" Johnnie said. "I can't wait to see him."

*   *   *   *

"Hi, Johnnie," Robyn said into the receiver. "Guess what?"

"I know, Kort's getting out of jail," Johnnie answered.

"Wow! That's great!" Robyn said. "But that isn't the news I have for you."

"So what's this big news?" Johnnie asked.

"The air conditioners at the Shoreline Motel are acting up because of all the heat we've had lately."

"Yeah, so what?" Johnnie said.

"So *what?*" Robyn asked, clearly surprised. "So this means my brother had to go into Mr. Owens' room a couple hours ago to fix his air conditioner."

"He did!?" Johnnie could hardly contain his excitement. "Did he find anything? Did he see anything? Does he know anything?"

Robyn laughed. "Well, he did see a scrapbook on the desk. And he just happened to 'accidentally-on-purpose' knock it off while trying to get to the air conditioner. And he happened to see that it was filled with newspaper and magazine clippings all about Kort."

"What were the articles about?" Johnnie asked.

"They dated back to the Vietnam War," Robyn said. "Josh didn't have time to read the articles but he noted some of the headlines. Basically, it looks like Mr. Owens was keeping track of Kort from Vietnam until now!"

"That is *really* weird. I mean, he never even contacted Kort until now!" Johnnie didn't like the sound of this at all. "Who else knows about this?" Johnnie asked.

"Josh, Tom, you and me, so far," said Robyn. "Josh and Tom are deciding if they should tell anyone else. I mean, it's not a *crime* to keep a scrapbook on someone you admire, is it?"

"I guess not," Johnnie said. "But I do think Kort should know. He'll be home this afternoon, and I think Josh and Tom should pay him a visit."

"Yes, I agree," Robyn said. "I'll let Josh know about Kort. What do *you* think this all means?"

"I don't even want to guess," Johnnie said. "Let's wait to hear what Kort has to say."

After Johnnie hung up the telephone, his mother came into the room. "Your dad drove over to the Arlington Home Healthcare store to talk with some of Kort's work friends. They've been taking care of

Kort's house while he's been in jail. They've arranged for all of us to go over there and put up some 'welcome home' decorations. I thought I'd bring over a casserole he could heat up for dinner too. Want to come?"

"Sure!" Johnnie said.

At Kort's house, the Jacobsons worked with Kort's friends to make sure the house would be ready for Kort's arrival. He was expected to be home at four o'clock that afternoon.

"Let's hang this 'welcome home' banner over the entryway into the dining room," said Mrs. Jacobson. "That way, it will be one of the first things he sees when he walks in the front door. See if you can find some tape, Johnnie."

Johnnie looked in the kitchen but couldn't find anything. Then he remembered Kort had an office. Sure enough, when Johnnie checked the middle desk drawer, the tape was there.

Soon, the house was decorated, the plants watered and Mrs. Jacobson's casserole was on the table. "We'd better leave now," Mrs. Jacobson said, looking at her watch. "It's 3:30 PM and he'll be home any minute now. Has everyone checked everything? Are all the plants watered and the rooms straightened?"

When Mrs. Jacobson was satisfied that everyone had done his or her job, she ushered everyone outside and closed the front door behind her.

"Boy, is *he* going to be surprised!" Johnnie said.

At about 4:30 PM the Jacobsons' phone rang. "Hello, Mrs. Jacobson? This is Kort. Say, I want to thank you for the delicious dinner you left for me. And the banner was an especially nice touch. The guys down at the shop tell me you were the one who planned the whole thing, and I just want you to know it means a lot to me. Hope you don't mind, but I invited them over for dinner!"

"Think nothing of it, Kort," Mrs. Jacobson answered. "I'm just glad we could do something nice for you after all you've been through so far."

Later that evening, the sounds of sirens nearby interrupted a television show Johnnie was watching. "Gee, I wonder what's going on?" he said. "It sounds like it's coming from a few streets behind us."

Johnnie wheeled himself out into their driveway. "Mom! Dad!" he yelled. "It looks like a fire!"

Mr. and Mrs. Jacobson joined their son outside. "It looks like it's coming from near Kort's house," Mrs. Jacobson said. The three of them looked at each other momentarily.

"Get in the car," Mr. Jacobson said.

When Johnnie and his family arrived on the street where the fire was, they could see that it was indeed Kort's house that was ablaze. It looked like the fire was contained but the Jacobsons could see that the house had been destroyed. Frantically, they looked for Kort.

"Look! There's a police cruiser," said Johnnie. "And look! There's Kort talking to a fireman. What's that thing the fireman is holding? It looks like some kind of gun!"

"Johnnie, you stay here while your mother and I go find out what's happening. There's too much commotion for you to try to make it over there in your wheelchair," Mr. Jacobson said.

Disappointed, Johnnie remained by the car while his parents carefully made their way over to Kort. He saw them talking to Kort and the fireman. Soon, the police officer who was in the cruiser joined them. Johnnie saw the fireman hold up the gun. Then he saw his mother shaking her head no.

"What's going on?" Johnnie moaned impatiently.

He didn't have to wait long for an answer. He saw his parents head back toward him. He rolled out to meet them.

"What's going on?" Johnnie called out. "Is Kort okay?"

Mr. Jacobson quickened his pace to meet his anxious son. "Yes, Kort's okay," he said. "But I think there's new evidence against Kort."

"Why? What do you mean?" Johnnie asked.

"When the firemen went into the house, one of them found a laser gun in Kort's office. He says it's not his, but—well, with all the talk about a laser setting off the bomb—"

"Wait a minute!" Johnnie shouted, interrupting his father. "*I* was in Kort's office—looking for tape. There wasn't any laser gun in there."

"Maybe he put it in there later," Mr. Jacobson said.

"No, I don't think so," Mrs. Jacobson said. "When he called me to thank me for the dinner, he mentioned that he had invited his friends from the shop over for dinner."

"Hmmm. And his friends *were* still there," Mr. Jacobson said. "Since his attorney drove him home and he apparently didn't go anywhere, it would be rather difficult to sneak a laser gun into his office, wouldn't you say?"

CHAPTER TEN

A Shadow in the Night

Mr. Jacobson rushed over to talk to the policeman and fire chief who were at the scene of the fire. In what seemed like a matter of minutes, the streets were filled with spectators. Television news cameras arrived along with the police chief.

"Hey Johnnie!" Danny yelled out. "What's going on?" Danny and Katy, along with their parents, were among the people who were wondering what all the commotion was about.

Johnnie quickly filled them in on what had happened. "My dad is telling the police about his suspicions that the laser gun was put in Kort's office by someone who wanted to get him into trouble."

"I think I'll go over there too," Mr. Randall said.

"Where's your mother, Johnnie?" Mrs. Randall asked. "I think I'll go keep her company."

Johnnie pointed her out in the crowd. Just then he spotted Travis riding toward them on his bicycle.

"Hi!" Travis called out. "I just saw Robyn and her parents walking down the sidewalk. And look! There's Joey and Nick."

Soon all the Gun Lake kids were standing together watching the fire fighters put out the blaze. Television crews busily set up cameras and lights as reporters scrambled to interview Kort, the police chief, the fire chief and a few witnesses.

Johnnie scanned the crowd looking for familiar faces. "Look!" he said, pointing toward the woods behind Kort's house. "I think I see somebody near one of those big trees behind the fence."

The kids strained to see where Johnnie was pointing. "It's really dark in there," Joey said. "I don't see anything but trees."

Johnnie looked again. "I *know* I saw someone," he said. "Keep looking."

"Hey! I saw something move from one tree to the next," Katy said.

I did too," Robyn said. "It looked like a man hiding in the shadows."

"Let's go check it out," Danny said.

"We can't go dressed like this," Travis said. "Most everyone here is wearing light colors. We'll be easy to spot. Besides, we can't just go in the woods unarmed."

"What are you thinking?" Danny asked.

"I say we go home, get on our camouflage clothes, pack up our laser guns and head for the woods," Travis replied.

"Our laser guns?!" Robyn said. "They're not real, Travis. I'm sure we're going to nail this guy with a toy gun. Maybe we could go up to him and say, 'Excuse me, sir. Would you mind putting on this laser pack so we can tag you?'"

Everyone but Travis laughed. "No, silly," he said, glaring at Robyn. "I *know* these are just toy guns—but *he* doesn't! They still shoot out a red light, don't they? If nothing else, it may scare him out of the woods. Then we can chase him out and get the police to arrest him."

"Arrest him for what?" Katy said. "For staring at a fire from the woods?"

"Katy's right," Johnnie said. "We don't know if this guy is any kind of threat. We can't jump to conclusions—believe me, I know!"

"Well, all right," Travis said. "But we can still have some fun. C'mon let's hurry up before it's all over."

The other kids looked at each other. Danny shrugged. "Why not? It'll be fun. I'll go tell my parents that we're going home. Johnnie, if you want me to, I'll help you get home. Then I'll go home and get ready before I come back to take you to the woods. Deal?"

"Deal!" Johnnie said. He was sure this was going to be fun. He saw his mother talking with Mrs. Randall, and wheeled over to them. "Danny's going to take me home and then we're going to play laser tag," he said. "It looks like the fire is almost out, anyway."

"Okay," Mrs. Jacobson said. "But stay out of trouble!"

Johnnie felt a little guilty as he and Danny left. "I told my mom we were going to play laser tag," Johnnie said. "I mean, I guess in a way we are."

"Well, when we get to the woods, we'll fire off a couple rounds at each other—so then you won't be lying," Danny said.

That made Johnnie feel better. And, even though he wouldn't have Danny's garage to hide in and the van mirrors to use, he was looking forward to playing laser tag in the dark.

In about 20 minutes, all the kids were ready and making their way to the woods that ran behind Kort's neighborhood.

"All right," Travis said in a hushed voice. "We're going to have to be as quiet as we can. Johnnie, I think if you stay on the dirt path, and push slowly, you'll be okay."

"I think we all need to stay together," Danny said.

As quietly as they could, the kids inched their way down the dark path. It was barely wide enough to accommodate Johnnie's chair. Joey helped push Johnnie, and Nick stayed close by. Travis led the way with Danny and the girls following him. They were close to the edge of the woods and could see the fire trucks and camera lights a few hundred feet ahead of them.

"Whoever is watching them, *if* he's still there, was in between Kort's house and the house next door," Robyn whispered.

Just then a twig snapped up ahead of them. The kids froze in their tracks. Travis motioned for everyone to crouch down.

"I think just one or two of us should go on ahead," Travis said in a hoarse whisper. "It would be too risky if all of us went. Whoever is up there might hear us."

Everyone agreed. Danny moved closer to Travis. "I'll go with you," he said quietly.

"Good!" Travis said.

Johnnie and the others watched as Travis and Danny faded into the shadows. "We'd better make sure we're well hidden too," Katy said. They all cautiously moved into the woods. Robyn helped

Johnnie get off the path and behind a tree trunk. They could still see the lights coming from in front of Kort's house. But they lost sight of Travis and Danny.

"I hope they'll be okay," Katy said.

"Me too!" Nick chimed in.

It seemed like hours went by before the kids heard or saw anything.

"Did you hear that?" Joey said.

"What?" Katy asked. "I didn't hear anything."

"It was sort of a sweeping sound," he said. He huddled closer to Robyn and Katy.

Everyone held their breath. Sure enough, there was a sound—like someone quietly brushing against dry leaves.

Johnnie's heart began pounding fast. He fought the impulse to shout, scream or yell. At the same time he found himself wanting to laugh. *This is just too spooky!* he thought to himself.

"Look! It's Danny!" Katy said aloud.

"Shhhh!" came the collective response.

Danny carefully walked, slightly bent over, to where the kids were hiding. Travis appeared just behind him.

"You're not going to believe what we saw," Danny said. "At first, all we could see were the lights from the cars, fire trucks and the cameras. Everything else looked like a silhouette."

"Yeah, at first I thought we wouldn't find anybody there," Travis said. "We had worked our way about 10 feet behind the fence so that we were looking through the trees out onto the street."

"Just then," Danny continued, "what we thought was a tree branch moved. And a man stepped out from behind the tree. His back was to us."

"But what *really* got our attention was what he was holding in his hand," Travis said.

"What was it?" Johnnie said, his voice trembling a little.

"A gun," Travis answered. "A *big* gun."

"It looked like a big *laser* gun," Danny added.

CHAPTER ELEVEN

Streaks of Light

"We've got to warn Kort!" Johnnie said. "Let's go tell the police."

"There's no time," Travis protested. "By the time we creep back out of the woods, go around the fence and make our way to Kort's house, this guy will either be gone or he will have shot someone."

"Well, what are we supposed to do?" Danny asked. "This guy has a weapon—a *laser* weapon."

"Yes, I know that," Travis said. "But I think we can create enough of a commotion that the police will have to investigate what's going on."

"Hmmm, I'm beginning to see what you mean," Johnnie said. "We need to come up with a plan that will draw the police's attention without getting us shot by this laser guy, whoever he is."

"I think I know who it is," Danny said. "I think it's Mr. Owens. He's the one who was acting so weird. The thing is *why* would he try to set up Kort? I thought they were army buddies."

"We don't have time to talk about that right now," Robyn said. "If we're going to come up with a plan, it had better be fast."

"I say we split up into three teams," Johnny said. "Nick, did you bring your walkie-talkie?"

"Sure did," Nick said proudly.

"And what about you, Joey?" Johnnie asked.

"It's on my belt," Joey said, patting it.

"I brought mine too," Johnnie said. "I keep it in my back pack for emergencies. So that means we have three walkie-talkies—one for each team."

"Good idea," Danny said. "I think Johnnie should be on team one with Robyn. Nick and Katy can go with me, and Joey, you're with Travis. Does that sound okay?"

"Fine with me," Travis said.

"Sounds good," Johnnie said.

"Travis, since you have just one partner with you, why don't you go over to the far right-hand side of where this guy is. Danny, I think you, Katy and Nick should be directly behind him. Robyn and I will stay on this side of him. We'll use the walkie-talkies to let each other know when we're in position."

"What happens when we're in position?" Robyn asked.

"Start firing your laser guns as fast as you can recharge them," Johnnie said. "Everybody ready?"

They all nodded.

"Then let's move out!"

Johnnie watched as Travis and Joey moved swiftly into the woods. They soon disappeared into the dark. Danny, Katy and Nick followed them. Robyn and Johnnie began to inch their way up the path.

Robyn leaned low and whispered into Johnnie's ear, "When we get to our spot, I think you should get out of your chair and lay on the ground. Sitting in a wheelchair—even if you're behind a tree—with a laser gun shooting at you just doesn't seem smart."

"Yeah, I know what you mean. I just hope we don't make too much noise."

Johnnie and Robyn had traveled about 15 feet when they saw the profile of the man. He was standing beside a tree, holding a gun. They could only see him from the waist up as bushes were blocking the rest of the view. Robyn placed a hand on Johnnie's shoulder. Silently, she indicated they'd better stop.

Johnnie carefully unbuckled his seat belt and, while Robyn held the chair steady, slithered out of the chair until he was sitting on the ground. Robyn backed the chair away and placed it beside a bush along the path. She grabbed the walkie-talkie and Johnnie's laser gun and carried them with her.

Johnnie laid down on the path and rolled over to his stomach. Using his arms, he crept army style into the woods. Robyn crouched down and duck-walked beside him so she could keep an eye on the man. Once, when the man seemed to look in their direction, Robyn caught her breath and put her hand on Johnnie's back, letting him know he should stop.

When they were in position, Johnnie took his walkie-talkie and pushed the talk button. Placing the mouthpiece close to his lips, Johnnie whispered, "J and R in position. Over."

No sound except a low crackle came back.

"They must still be getting in their positions," Robyn whispered.

Again, the man looked in their direction. Johnnie put his fingers to his lips, and the two of them remained very still.

About two minutes slipped by before Johnnie's walkie-talkie made a small popping sound. Johnnie quickly adjusted the volume to its lowest setting. "D, K and N in position. Over." The sound was barely audible, but Johnnie knew he couldn't risk having it any louder.

Travis' voice indicating he and Joey were in position followed about 30 seconds after Danny's check-in.

Just then Robyn looked up. "He's gone!" she whispered to Johnnie.

Johnnie pushed himself up onto his elbows. Quickly, he clicked the talk button. "Can any of you see him? J and R have lost visual contact."

"D, K and N can see him. He's moving toward you, Johnnie!"

Travis clicked on. "We've got to shoot— NOW!"

Taking a deep breath, Johnnie raised his gun to his shoulders and began firing his laser. A red streak of light burst forward into the trees. Robyn, likewise began firing. She was trembling so hard that most of her laser fire was aimed toward the treetops.

Soon, Johnnie could see small streaks of red light coming from all directions. It looked as if all the "laser fire" was coming from the toy guns.

Suddenly, a much brighter streak of red split the night air and set a pile of leaves on fire near the place where Johnnie and Robyn hid.

"What do we do?" Robyn said, panicking.

"Keep firing!" Johnnie yelled.

Suddenly, the forest erupted in streams of red

light and loud yells from the kids. "If this doesn't get Kort's attention, I don't know what will," Johnnie said.

"Hey! What's going on in there!" Johnnie heard someone yell. "Where are all those red lights coming from?"

Just then another solid red beam of light hit a tree branch just above Johnnie's head, sending charred twigs down to the ground.

The next sound Johnnie heard was the hurried footsteps of police officers and rescue workers running toward the fence. "Aim those camera lights into the woods," someone shouted.

Soon the woods became flooded in light. Eerie, long shadows sprawled across the path. Johnnie heard the sound of running footsteps heading their way. He could hear the shouts of the other kids as they joined several police officers in the chase.

Robyn and Johnnie remained still. The footsteps became louder and suddenly the man's army fatigues came into view. From their hiding spot, Johnnie and Robyn could see Mr. Owens running down the path toward the end of the fence.

As soon as he was past them, Robyn stood up and scrambled to retrieve Johnnie's chair. She saw a policeman running toward her. "He's heading for the street!" she yelled, pointing in the direction he had gone.

Soon Danny, Katy and the others caught up to Robyn and Johnnie. Johnnie climbed back into his chair just as Kort came running down the path toward them. "What are you guys doing?" he yelled.

"It was Mr. Owens," Travis said. "He had a laser gun and was watching you from the woods. We didn't realize he had a gun until we got in the woods. So we decided to get your attention."

"Well, you sure did that! Do you realize what a dangerous thing you just did? If that really was a laser gun he was carrying, you could have been killed."

"Oh, it was real, all right," Robyn said. She pointed to the still-smoldering leaves."

Kort stomped out the remaining burning embers. "I'd better join the police and find out what this is all about," he said. "And you guys stay put until he's caught. That's an order!"

"Yessir!" Johnnie said. He was glad this adventure was just about over.

"Well, I guess we ended up playing laser tag after all," Danny said to Johnnie.

"Yeah, that was the wildest game of tag I've ever played," Johnnie replied.

"And by the looks of how close that laser fire came to you, you were almost 'it'," Joey said.

"We've got to get a little closer," Travis said, "or we're never going to know when they catch Mr. Owens."

The kids could hear shouts and footsteps running through the woods. One of the police officers who was chasing Mr. Owens had used his walkie-talkie to ask for assistance. Johnnie could see four police cars blocking off the side street that led to the street Kort's house was on. The side street ended at the edge of the woods. Already policemen and police dogs were in the woods, chasing Mr. Owens.

"Well, I guess we could move a *little* closer," Johnnie said. "But Kort warned us to stay away until Mr. Owens is caught—and after I saw what his laser gun did to the leaves and the branch, I think he's right"

The others agreed, so they slowly made their way down the path toward the hub of all the search activity.

Johnnie heard more shouting. Then he saw the unmistakable red stream of light come from Mr.

Owens' laser. A gunshot followed that.

"We got him!" an officer yelled.

Johnnie and the others took off as fast as they could toward the scene. Kort ran to meet them. "It's all over," Kort said, breathing hard.

"Did—did they *kill* him?" Nick asked.

Kort knelt down and gave Nick a big hug. "No, Nick, they didn't kill him. They just wounded him."

"Why did he do it?" Johnnie asked.

"That's what we still have to find out," Kort answered.

"Do you think Mr. Faraday or Scott hired him to blow up the car and then frame you?" Robyn asked.

"At this point, I can't say," Kort answered. "I don't *want* to believe that either Chester or Scott could do something like that, but I guess *anything* is possible."

"Well, one thing for sure," Johnnie said. "*You* didn't do it. You're in the clear now, right?"

"I'm not totally in the clear," Kort said. "It will all depend on what Mr. Owens has to say."

CHAPTER TWELVE

Confession

The next morning, Johnnie awoke with a start. He remembered the look on Mr. Owens' face when the police led him to the police cruiser. "He looks like a very bitter man," his mother had remarked.

When the laser fire started, Johnnie's and Robyn's parents were sure that the kids were somehow involved in something more than just tag, and alerted Kort to what was going on. The distinct red laser beam from Mr. Owens' gun tipped off Kort that something serious was happening.

"We were all so afraid for you," Mrs. Jacobson had said.

But that was last night. What would today bring? Johnnie couldn't wait for Kort to call them and let them know what Mr. Owens' story was.

At the breakfast table, Mr. Jacobson sipped on some coffee while reading the Sunday morning paper. "I'm afraid the local paper won't pick up on the story until tomorrow," he said. "One thing, though, that struck me as odd last night. Before Mr. Owens got into the police cruiser, he turned to Kort and said, 'Looks like you escaped another grenade.' I wonder what he meant by that?"

"All I know is," Johnnie said, "Mr. Owens was awfully interested in Kort. While Josh Anderson was fixing the air conditioner in Mr. Owens' motel room, he discovered a scrapbook. It had pictures and articles all about Kort, from his early military career until recently."

"I'm sure the police will go through Mr. Owens' room very carefully, looking for information," Mr. Jacobson said.

* * * *

At about three o'clock that afternoon, the Jacobsons received a telephone call from Kort. "I don't know where to begin," he said. "The police found a scrapbook all about me in Owens' room. They also found some laser-making parts—including a few self-adhesive labels that he or someone had printed off on a computer. The labels, which are supposed to be affixed to any laser product, contained the standard warning about possible radiation harm.

"They also found maps of the area. One map had a circle around the area where the Faraday garage is located. And they found a notepad that had notes of a telephone conversation with Mr. Faraday. He even had Mr. Faraday's private telephone number written on it."

"Oh, dear," Mrs. Jacobson said, when she heard the news. "This is *not* looking good for Mr. Faraday. But at least it looks like Kort can be cleared of all charges."

Johnnie was glad that the police would probably drop the charges against Kort, but it troubled him that Mr. Faraday might somehow be involved.

It wasn't until mid-afternoon on Monday that news broke about Mr. Owens' confession. Kort drove over to the Jacobsons' house that evening. As he walked in the front door, his face told the whole story.

"I'm free!" he beamed. "It's all over."

"What happened?" Johnnie asked.

"It all started back in Cambodia, when Nathaniel Owens saved my life. While he was recuperating from his injuries, he learned that I had been promoted to lieutenant. He was sure he was going to be promoted too, but when that didn't happen, he became bitter.

"He blamed me for his leg being amputated because, in saving my life, the grenade shattered his leg. He also blamed me for 'ruining' his military career. And he has been blaming me for everything that has gone wrong in his life ever since."

"Was he trying to *kill* you at the Faradays' race track?" Johnnie asked.

"No, he didn't want to kill me. He just wanted to ruin me like I supposedly ruined him."

"Well, how does Mr. Faraday enter into the picture?" Mrs. Jacobson asked.

"For a few years, Owens lost track of me. When I became the Faradays' chief mechanic, I was interviewed a couple of times for some racing magazines—especially after Chester's accident. People were interested in what he was doing. Anyway, Owens saw one of the articles and began following my career again. When he saw that Scott was on a losing streak, and that the Faradays were losing money, he called Chester Faraday and offered to destroy the racer so he could get the insurance money."

"And Mr. Faraday *let* him!?" Johnnie asked.

"According to Mr. Faraday, he politely but firmly told Mr. Owens that he was not interested," Kort said.

"Does Mr. Faraday have any way of backing up his story?" Mr. Jacobson asked.

"Apparently, after Mr. Owens called him with the offer, Mr. Faraday told his attorney about it," Kort said.

"Then why didn't Mr. Faraday say something when you were arrested?" Mrs. Jacobson said.

"Because, when Owens called Chester, he told him he was a friend of mine, and that I had given him Chester's phone number," Kort answered. "So, in Chester's mind, I was somehow involved."

"Wow!" said Johnnie. "It all makes sense now."

"And what Mr. Owens said about you escaping another grenade makes sense too," Mr. Jacobson added. "Only this time, *he* was the one who was trying to hurt you."

"I'm just glad it's all over," Johnnie said. "What are you going to do now, Kort?"

"Well, Mr. Faraday told me that he's going to use the insurance money to build another car, and that he wants me to stay on as chief mechanic."

"I'll bet Scott isn't too happy about that," Johnnie said.

"Actually, Scott is *very* happy about that. It seems that because of all the publicity about the car and how Scott didn't really like racing, another young racer has asked to join the team. Scott will be able to enjoy racing as a spectator—and, who knows, maybe he'll get some of his songs published."

"Cool!" said Johnnie.

"As for you and the kids," Kort said. "I want to thank you for believing in me. If it hadn't been for your fast thinking, I might still be going to jail. Do you think you and the others have had enough excitement for one summer?"

Johnnie smiled. "Well, maybe for *this* summer. But fall is coming, and who knows what will happen."

Alternatives in Motion

A portion of the proceeds from sales of The Gun Lake Adventure Series goes to support the nonprofit organization Alternatives in Motion, founded by Johnnie Tuitel in 1995. The mission of Alternatives in Motion is to provide wheelchairs to individuals who do not qualify for other assistance and who could not obtain such equipment without financial aid.

If you would like to help out and make a donation please, send a check made out to Alternatives in Motion to the address below.

For further information please see our web site or contact Johnnie Tuitel at Alternatives in Motion. Please call if you would like to arrange to have Johnnie Tuitel speak at your event or school.

Alternatives in Motion
1916 Breton Road SE
Grand Rapids, MI 49506
616.493.2620 (voice)
616.493.2621 (fax)
877.468.9335 (voice toll free)
www.alternativesinmotion.org

Alternatives in Motion is a nonprofit 501(c) (3) organization

From Fox Lake Press, Chicago

"Teaching your children about disabilities just got easier thanks to The Gun Lake Adventure Series."

From the Children's Bookwatch—Midwest Book Review:

"...A pure delight for young readers, *Discovery on Blackbird Island* is the third volume in "The Gun Lake Adventure Series," and like its predecessors, *The Barn at Gun Lake* and *Mystery Explosion!*, showcases the substantial storytelling talents of Johnnie Tuitel and Sharon Lamson.

"The fourth in Cedar Tree Publishing's outstanding "Gun Lake Adventure" series, *Searching the Noonday Trail* is another great novel by Johnnie Tuitel and Sharon Lamson for young readers which is wonderfully written and totally entertaining from first page to last."

"A most enjoyable and entertaining story, *Adventure in the Bear Tooth Mountains* is a welcome and commended addition to school and community libraries."

From the Grand Rapids Press:

"...(the) Gun Lake Adventure Series is capturing the attention of young readers in Grand Rapids and beyond."

From the Statesman Journal, Salem, OR:

"A fine Series for all children, who can have the fun of an adventure while learning that "different" doesn't mean inferior or threatening."

From WE Magazine:

"An excellent venture."

Gun Lake Adventure Series

by Johnnie Tuitel and Sharon Lamson
For young readers ages 8-12

The Barn at Gun Lake (1998, Cedar Tree Publishing, $5.99 paperback, **Book 1, ISBN 0-9658075-0-9**
The Gun Lake kids stumble upon some modern pirates when they find an illegal copy of popular CDs in a deserted barn. While solving the mystery, there is a boat chase and then a dangerous wheelchair chase through the woods.

Mystery Explosion! (1999, Cedar Tree Publishing, $5.99 paperback, **Book 2, ISBN 0-9658075-1-7**
First there is an explosion. Then an arrest is made that shocks the quiet town of Gun Lake. A stranger in town and a search for his identity paves the way for another fast-paced mystery. Friendship and loyalties are tested as Johnnie Jacobson and his friends try to find the answers to "Who did it?" and "Why?"

Discovery on Blackbird Island (2000, Cedar Tree Publishing, $5.99 paperback, **Book 3, ISBN 0-9658075-2-5**
Blackbird Island is a small, quiet uninhabited island in Gun Lake. Or is it? A disturbing discovery sends Johnnie Jacobson and his friends on yet another Gun Lake adventure filled with schemes, action and mysteries to solve.

Searching the Noonday Trail (2000, Cedar Tree Publishing, $5.99 paperback, **Book 4, ISBN 0-9658075-3-3)**
***(Selected for inclusion in *'Outstanding Books for Young People with Disabilities"* by IBBY (International Board on Books for Young People 2005) compiled through the Documentation Centre of Books for Disabled Young People, Oslo, Norway, **www.ibby.org)** Summer's over and Johnnie is nervous about going to a new school. Will it be as adventuresome as the summer was? Johnnie's not too sure. But a secret football play and a field trip to where Chief Noonday and the Ottawa tribe used to live put Johnnie and his Gun Lake friends hot on the trail of another exciting adventure.

Adventure in the Bear Tooth Mountains (2003, Cedar Tree Publishing, $5.99 paperback, **Book 5, ISBN 0-9658075-4-1)** A three-family Christmas vacation to the Bear Tooth Mountains in Montana test Johnnie and his friends' survival skills. Ghost towns, a mysterious old man, a blizzard and a mountain lion pave the road to challenges and daring.

The Light in Bradford Manor (2004, Cedar Tree Publishing, $5.99 paperback, **Book 6, ISBN 0-9658075-5-X**) Johnnie and his friends are treated to a special two-week adventure at Camp Riley in Indiana. There, Johnnie and his friends from Michigan and some of his newfound friends from Camp Riley find themselves on a hunt to solve a mystery – one that involves the legendary ghost of Bradford Manor.

For more information visit www.cedartreepublishing.org

Johnnie Tuitel *who has cerebral palsy and uses a wheelchair, is a much sought-after speaker nationally. He motivates and inspires students of all ages, business people and community leaders with his often humorous and real-life stories. Johnnie, his wife Deb and their three sons live in Grand Rapids, Michigan.*

Sharon Lamson *has been a freelance writer for over twenty years. She is also the author of several children's books and curriculum for both children and adults. She has been published with Tommy Nelson Publishers, Zondervan Publishing and with Cedar Tree Publishing as co-author of their own Gun Lake Adventure Series. Sharon and her husband Robert live in Norton Shores, Michigan. They have five grown children.*